THE BIG
FAIL

ALSO AVAILABLE:

MICAH'S GOT TALENT?

COMING SOON:

TO SKETCH A THIEF

JUST CHILL

MICAH'S SUPER VLOG! THE BIG FAIL

BY ANDY MCGUIRE

ILLUSTRATIONS BY GIRISH MANUEL

Copyright ©2019 by Hachette Book Group
Published in association with JellyTelly Press

Cover copyright ©2019 by Hachette Book Group

FaithWords is a division of Hachette Book Group, Inc. The FaithWords name and logo are trademarks of Hachette Book Group, Inc.

JellyTelly Press is a division of Winsome Truth, Inc.

FaithWords
Hachette Book Group
1290 Avenue of the Americas, New York, NY 10104

hachettebookgroup.com | faithwords.com | jellytelly.com

Micah's Super Vlog trademark and character rights are owned by Square One World Media, Inc., and used by permission. Micah's Super Vlog was created by Girish Manuel for Square One World Media.

Written by Andy McGuire
Illustrated by Girish Manuel
Layout by Sarah Siegand

First Edition: June 2019

Scripture quotations marked ESV are from the ESV® Bible (The Holy Bible, English Standard Version®), copyright ©2001 by Crossway, a publishing ministry of Good News Publishers. Used by permission. All rights reserved.

Scripture quotations marked GW are taken from GOD'S WORD Translation (GW) Copyright ©1995 by God's Word to the Nations. Used by permission of Baker Publishing Group.

Scripture quotations marked ICB are taken from The Holy Bible, International Children's Bible® Copyright ©1986, 1988, 1999, 2015 by Tommy Nelson™, a division of Thomas Nelson. Used by permission.

Scripture quotations marked MSG are taken from The Message (MSG) Copyright ©1993, 1994, 1995, 1996, 2000, 2001, 2002 by Eugene H. Peterson.

Scripture quotations marked NLT are taken from the Holy Bible, New Living Translation, copyright ©1996, 2004, 2015 by Tyndale House Foundation. Used by permission of Tyndale House Publishers, Inc., Carol Stream, Illinois 60188. All rights reserved.

Scripture quotations marked NLV are taken from the New Life Version (NLV) Copyright ©1969, 2003 by Barbour Publishing, Inc.

Library of Congress Cataloging-in-Publication Data has been applied for.

ISBN: 978-1-5460-3464-3 (trade paperback), 978-1-5460-3354-7 (hardcover), 978-1-5460-3463-6 (ebook)

Printed in the USA.
LSC-C
10 9 8 7 6 5 4 3 2 1

For my wonderful son, Charlie, who loves history enough to NOT make it up on the spot.

– AM

To Nikki, Always be yourself and nobody else.

– GM

CHAPTER ONE

Just before the bell rang, the kids in Micah Murphy's fifth-grade classroom headed to their seats. Their teacher, Mr. Turtell, wasn't there yet, so everyone talked among themselves.

Micah and his classmates were surprised that Mr. Turtell wasn't sitting at his desk, waiting for class to begin promptly on time—he was the strictest teacher in all of New Leaf Elementary. Mr. Turtell would *never* be late. Mr. Turtell wouldn't normally undermine the authority of the tardy bell like this. *What on earth could have happened this morning?*

Surprising as it was that their teacher was MIA, there was only one topic of conversation as the students waited for Mr. Turtell to arrive: tomorrow's local history test.

"I heard it's going to be hard," said Liam.

"I heard it's going to be *really* hard!" said Abby.

"I heard it has questions about stuff from the beginning of the school year!" said Katie.

"I heard it has questions about stuff Mr. Turtell hasn't even taught us yet!" said Mara.

"I heard it has questions about history that hasn't even happened yet!" added Chet.

Mr. Turtell still hadn't arrived, so the kids got louder and more excited, each trying to one-up the other.

"I heard even history teachers would get an F on it!" said Eric.

"I heard even Albert Einstein would get an F on it!" said Akira.

"I heard even the guy at the state fair who guesses people's age and weight would get an F on it!" said Gabe. "And he knows everything!"

No one knew how to top that one.

"Well, *I'm* not going to get an F," said Armin. "I'm going to study for three hours straight!"

"Oh, yeah?" said Hanz. "I'm going to drink five cups of coffee and study all night!"

"I'm studying right now!" said Lydia.

By this point everyone in the entire classroom had said something about the test. Well, almost everyone.

All eyes turned to Micah, who was doodling on his notebook cover. He was trying to draw a Captain Karate Dino Cop from his *Captain Karate Dino Cop* game, but it was hard to get the triceratops judo chop stance just right. He looked up.

"Sorry—did I miss something?"

Armin sighed. "We're talking about tomorrow's big history test. You want to study with Lydia, Gabe, and me?"

"Why? Is it supposed to be hard?" Micah asked.

The whole class burst out laughing. Micah knew it was at him, but he didn't get the joke.

Mr. Turtell walked into the classroom just as the bell rang. "Have a seat, everyone," he said, despite the fact that everyone was already in their chairs. He placed his turtle-shaped lunch box in the drawer of his turtle-covered desk and hung his jacket on a turtle-decorated coat hook on the wall.

Mr. Turtell's classroom was the weirdest in the whole school, which was quite a feat, since Miss

Tibby's room had real live snakes and tarantulas in it! Picture the way your yard looks in autumn, when the leaves fall from the trees so fast and thick you can't see an inch of the ground anymore. Mr. Turtell's classroom was exactly like that, only instead of leaves, it was turtles.

They were everywhere!

There were turtles of all makes and models: box, sea, snapping, ninja. Some made of plastic, some glass, some clay. Several were made of things that used to be edible but weren't anymore. If you weren't careful, your eyes would wander from turtle to turtle like a crazy game of connect-the-dots.

Why so many turtles? Because every mother of every student Mr. Turtell had ever had thought his name was pronounced "Mr. Turtle" instead of "Mr. Tur-TELL," and not one student had ever bothered to correct them. And there's nothing moms of elementary school students like more than giving clever Christmas gifts to their kids' teachers. Year after year, the turtles piled up until they grew into a plague. And now it was too late to do anything about it. The turtles had won.

But Micah liked turtles, so he didn't mind. Although they did make it harder to pay attention in class.

"I hope you all remember that you have a history test tomorrow," Mr. Turtell said. "It will be on local history, which is of course the best history of all. When it comes to history, the loccaller, the better."

Lydia's hand shot up.

"Don't say it," Armin whispered. "Never correct a teacher."

"But that's not even a real word!" Lydia whispered back.

Armin glared. Lydia put her hand back down.

"The test will count as a third of your final grade for the semester," Mr. Turtell went on. "It will cover the history of Middletown from the pre-Colonial muskrat trappers, through the outhouse manufacturing boom of the 1800s, all the way up to the Great Sewage Backup of 2012."

Akira raised her hand. "Will there be any questions about Mr. Henry, Middletown's oldest man? I heard he's a hundred and fifty-two!"

"I don't think so," said Mr. Turtell.

"You don't think he's a hundred and fifty-two, or you don't think there'll be a question about him on the test?"

"Both."

"Will there be a question about why the town always smells like rotten cantaloupe?" Timothy asked.

"Unlikely," said Mr. Turtell.

"Will there be any questions about Mayor Kim getting food poisoning from a bad tamale?" Luciana asked.

"Definitely not," said Mr. Turtell.

"How about an essay on the founding of Pukey Pete's CoasterTown?" Gabe asked.

"Not a chance," said Mr. Turtell.

"How about a question about the time the fireworks factory burned down?" Eric asked.

"Absolutely!" said Mr. Turtell. "Best fireworks show ever!"

That evening, Micah told his parents about the big test, and they let him study right after dinner instead of having to load the dishwasher.

Micah looked around his room. It turned out the dishes weren't the only things that needed cleaning. He'd never be able to focus in this mess, so he figured he'd start with the floor and work his way up from there. He didn't even recognize half the clothes that were piled on the carpet. Were they somebody else's, or were they so dirty their original colors couldn't be determined?

The phone rang. Micah ran to get it.

"Hello?"

"Hey, Micah."

"Hey, Armin."

"You sure you don't want to study with me and Lydia?"

"No, I'll be fine." He hated studying with Lydia. All she ever did was ask them questions from her notes, and they never even took breaks for snacks or video games!

"Okay. Good luck!"

"You too. Bye."

Talking to Armin reminded him that he could probably use a quick video game break after all his room cleaning. It would help him get focused. He put in *Captain Karate Dino Cop* and started at level 7, right outside the crime den of the Stegosaurus Boys. He needed to get inside to grab evidence against them if he ever wanted to take the whole gang down for good.

After only fourteen attempts to get by the den's raptor guards, he decided he should probably get back to work. He grabbed his notebook from his backpack, sat down at his desk, and looked out the window to gather his thoughts. It was a beautiful night, with clear skies and gentle breezes. Had that tree always been there? It looked new. And what about that squirrel? Yeah, he was pretty sure he'd never seen that squirrel before. It was probably visiting from out of town.

The setting sun was shining through Micah's window, so he looked back down at his desk. To his left was the Lego model of the rocket train he'd been working on for three weeks. He was so close to being done with it, except there was one little gray piece missing. He knew if he could just find that last piece—it had probably fallen on his rug and blended in—he could put the model up on his shelf and it wouldn't distract him anymore.

He got on his hands and knees and brushed his fingers through the plush rug, feeling for anything hard. He found a toothpick, some dried-up Play-Doh, three thumbtacks, the left foot of an action figure, and an uncooked macaroni noodle. No Legos.

He got under his desk and felt around with his hands in the dark. Mostly dust bunnies and spiderwebs. Ouch! Did something bite him? Wait! There was something pointy and plastic in the back corner. Ha! He'd found it! Now he could complete the rocket train! There was no stopping him now! He put the last piece on the side of the engine

and gently placed the train on the top shelf of his bookcase.

At last! He could study in peace. He opened up his notebook.

Huh. When had he made that sketch of a laser blaster? It wasn't very good. The proportions were way off, and what was that weird contraption on the side supposed to be?

Micah ripped the page out of his notebook, crumpled it up, and threw it at his trash can. He missed. He ripped out another page and crumpled it up too. Another miss.

The garbage can was too far away, all the way back in the farthest corner of his room. Maybe he should stop playing paper wad basketball and switch to paper wad Frisbee golf. Then he could see if he could make the shot in three tosses. But he'd need a smaller hole than a trash can, or it would be too easy.

Luckily, he had an old milkshake cup on his nightstand from the week before last. And it was mostly empty too! He started at the farthest corner from his nightstand and took a shot. So close! It bounced off the rim and landed on the floor. From there he could make it in only one more shot. That was one less than his goal!

He should probably get back to studying now. Enough of a break. He sat back down at his desk and turned to a page of his notes that didn't have any drawings on it. Just words. Boring words. He read several of them. A dozen, perhaps. He needed something to make this interesting. But what?

He stood up and paced as he read, so he wouldn't get sleepy from boredom. He paced faster and faster, until the words were blurry and he couldn't read them. He needed to go slower but still keep it interesting.

The floor is lava! That's it! It was a game he used to play with Armin when they were little. They'd pretend the floor was made of burning-hot lava, and if they stepped on it, their feet would melt. So, they could only step on couches and tables and chairs and anything else off the floor. (Obviously, this was not a game you played when parents were around.)

Micah stood up on his bed, with his notebook open. As he read, he walked across his mattress and stepped onto his end table. Then, still staring at his notebook, he headed for his desk. After his desk, he'd have to hold on to the curtain rod as he shimmied across the skinny windowsill. No problem. He just needed to grab the rod with one hand while holding the notebook open with the other.

Easy enough. He used to hold on to the rod and walk the window all the time—when he was younger. And lighter.

Crack!

Was that the sound of drywall breaking?

Down came the curtain rod, still in Micah's hand. His foot slipped off the windowsill. Micah nearly lost his balance, but leaned forward, just catching himself against the highest shelf of his bookcase. When it started to tip forward, Micah tried to push it back.

No luck.

He crashed to the floor.

Micah lay there in a daze, staring up at the top

shelf as it collapsed. Down fell his rocket train, followed by a Lego biplane. Each crashed to the ground in a heap of small plastic parts. Then came the next shelf, with his comic books. And last but not least, his video camera and vlog equipment.

On his back, in a pile of his own stuff, he heard his mother walking down the hall.

She opened the door. "Are you all right?"

"I think so."

"What a mess! You really need to clean up in here!"

"Sorry, Mom. I will."

Micah sat up and looked around. He started picking stuff off the floor. Yep, he would just clean up his room really quick and then get right back to studying.

Suddenly he felt the strangest sense of déjà vu.

Study Much?

How did I spend the entire night cleaning my room (twice)?! I haven't even looked at my history notes since flying off the curtain rod a few hours ago! What's wrong with me? Why can't I be more like Lydia—someone who loves to study and learn? Nope. I'm just lazy ole Micah, who would rather play Lava Floor than read about the history of my town.

I'm always completely distracted when I study. WHOA. What was that? I think I just saw a squirrel ninja flip over a bird! So cool . . . Wait a second—what was I talking about?

Anyways, everyone said this test is going to be hard. I'll never be ready now. I'd better get some sleep. I have to get up at the crack of dawn to review my history notes (if I can find any in my notebook).

Whatever work you do,
do it with all your heart.
Do it for the Lord.
Colossians 3:23 (NLV)

▷ **When it comes to studying, are YOU a Micah or a Lydia?**

▷ **What do YOU think Micah should do to stay focused?**

CHAPTER TWO

Suddenly, spaceships were shooting lasers at Micah. For some reason he couldn't remember how he'd gotten into this space war in the first place. And what kind of aliens was he fighting against? Or maybe *he* was the alien?

His eyes opened and he looked up at the ceiling.

Phew! It was all just a dream. But that means the noise wasn't lasers—it was his alarm.

Nuts!

How long had it been going off? He looked at the clock. 7:15?!?

He'd planned to get up early and study, since he

never got the chance the night before. His parents had already left for work. If *they* could see him now! He hadn't studied *and* he'd overslept. And now he only had fifteen minutes to get to school!

Oh, well. He'd just have to take a few shortcuts in his "getting ready" routine. Okay. Concentrate. Just the essentials.

First step: put on pants.

Yep. That pretty much covered the essentials.

Showers were skippable. Breakfast was skippable. Toothbrushing was skippable.

He should probably put on a shirt, though. Not as crucial as pants, but still.

He walked down the hall toward the front door, grabbing his backpack. His sister, Audrey, was sitting at the kitchen table, staring at him. "Running late?"

"Yep."

"Good job remembering your pants."

"Thanks."

Micah got to his classroom just as the bell rang.

Armin and Lydia were already in their seats.

"How long did you study?" Lydia asked.

"Umm . . ."

Armin shook his head in disappointment. "You never got around to studying, did you?"

"Well . . ."

"What were you thinking?" Lydia asked.

"I . . ."

"I just don't get you," Armin said.

"Er . . ."

"Can you even use any actual words?" Lydia asked.

"Uhhh . . ."

Mr. Turtell walked in just then. "Put your books and notebooks away," he said, "and get out a pen or pencil. You'll have all class period to take this test, so take your time. It's time to get historical!"

As the tests were passed down the rows, Micah took a deep breath. It would be fine, right? After all, what was the worst that could happen? He could fail. Big deal. It's not like he'd have to go back and repeat the fifth grade—or worse, the fourth grade. They can't do that, can they? He'd be behind all his friends. On the flip side, at least in fourth grade you got to go to the zoo for your field trip instead of the ballet. And maybe he'd get to make another one of those popsicle stick log cabins. That was fun.

But even a popsicle stick log cabin wasn't worth having to make all new friends and having a permanent blemish on his record. He'd better do well on this test. He just hoped he could remember some things from his teacher's lectures.

Not likely. So many distractions. So many turtles.

Micah looked through the questions. Nuts. It was all essays. At least with multiple choice and true-false questions, you could get lucky and guess your way to a few right answers. With essays you had to bluff it. Micah was not typically good at making stuff up.

Question 1: Describe the origins of the city of Middletown. *Okay*, Micah thought to himself. *Just ask yourself who, what, when, and why questions. Who founded it? What used to be there? When did they found it? Why did people move there?*

Micah stared up at the ceiling to think. It took him several minutes to collect himself but, for better or worse, thoughts started coming to him.

Question 2: What role did Middletown play in the Civil War?

Once again Micah had to pause to think. What did he know about the Civil War, anyway? Not much. But based on the name, it sounded like one of the nicer wars. His mom always told Audrey, "Be civil to your brother," which basically meant be polite and stop saying so many nasty things.

Something about the answer he wrote down didn't feel quite right to Micah, but it was the best he could think of under pressure.

Question 3: Describe a leading industry in Middletown today.

Uh-oh. Micah was totally blank. He couldn't think of anything. He remembered Mr. Turtell was always going on and on about natural resources. Maybe that would help. But what natural resources did Middletown have?

Micah was always seeing squirrels around. Were they a resource? What would you do with them? Could you make them into a hat? That didn't sound right.

Didn't he remember Mr. Turtell saying something about outhouse manufacturing? But that was probably not a big business anymore. He didn't see a lot of outhouses around, unless you counted Port-a-Pottys at the county fair.

Maybe he should think through the jobs of the people he knew. His dad was an accountant, but Micah

A Test by Micah Murphy

1. What is the video game store of choice for all true gamers?

   ANSWER: Vern's Video Games and More. It is one of the oldest and most-respected establishments in town, founded all the way back in the early '90s. Talk about historical!

2. What is Vern's best-selling product?

   ANSWER: Cheez-um Niblet Crunchers—the gamer snack food of choice. Gives you the energy boost you need without the crash of sugary foods. Plus, the crumbs are greasy enough to slide right through the crevices in gaming controls without gunking them up!

3. Where did Mayor Kim get his bad tamale?

   ANSWER: Chip's Down-Home Authentic Mexican Cuisine, a food truck parked in the alley behind the SaveMore Market. (Tip: avoid the tamales, but their Szechuan chicken is surprisingly good!)

didn't think that counted as an industry. Accountants didn't make anything. Industries make stuff.

Micah's mom volunteered at the food pantry. No, that's not an industry. That's a ministry.

But wait! What about his sister's job? That was the future!

Micah wrote as quickly as he could. Time was almost up, but luckily Micah was nearly to the end. It was amazing that there wasn't one question he was sure he knew the answer to. Where were all the facts about the stuff in Middletown that actually mattered?

Time was up. Mr. Turtell collected the tests and dismissed the students to their reading groups. Micah caught up to Armin, Lydia, and Gabe. He was almost afraid to ask, but couldn't help himself.

"Well, what did you guys think?"

"That was so hard!" Gabe confessed. "I don't feel good."

"Yeah, it was really tough," Armin said.

Lydia glared at Micah. "But not so bad if you studied."

Hanz came up behind them. "Vell, I zought it vas as easy as a piece of pie."

Gabe suddenly ran off, holding his stomach. "Gotta find a bathroom! Or a garbage can! Or a hat!"

Essay Questions?!

Sometimes I wonder if there's a secret association of teachers who laugh about how bad they stump their students on all essay question tests. Why else would they taunt us with those blank spaces? To make fools of us, that's why!

I think I did my best . . . and by "best" I mean completely fabricating my answers. I had no idea what I was writing about! What am I going to do if I fail this test? Ugh . . . I should have spent time studying AND praying instead of playing video games last night. I know God is always near and will help me when I ask Him to.

"My grace is all you need. My power works best in weakness."
2 Corinthians 12:9 (NLT)

▷ **How could God have helped Micah if he'd asked?**

▷ **Can YOU remember a time God helped you when you prayed?**

CHAPTER THREE

The next morning, on the way to school, Micah was a nervous wreck. He and his classmates would be getting their tests back, and his emotions were all over the place. Sometimes he felt a wave of confidence. After all, it was possible he'd done all right on it.

But that passed quickly, followed by a wave of fear so strong it was like he'd just gotten punched in the stomach. It was as if he was right on the precipice of some horrible disaster, like when a huge storm blows into your neighborhood and your WiFi goes out for, like, three hours.

As Micah walked, he decided to hum to keep his mind off the test. He thought about trying to match his mood with the Downers' newest hit, "Eating Cold Cereal in the Dark." But that would probably just bring him lower.

No, he needed something peppy. He hated to admit it, but a song by Lydia's favorite band, the Dreem Doodz, would be perfect. He started to sing "Mmmm Yeah Yeah, That's Right, Yeah" but then realized he had gotten it mixed up with their other smash hit, "Yeah, Yeah, Mmm Mmm, Don't You Know It, Yeah."

Yep, that was the one he needed. He started to get his groove back just as he headed into his classroom.

As Micah sat down at his desk, he could overhear everyone talking about the test. They were comparing answers, trying to figure out which ones they'd got right. Micah listened in to several conversations but didn't hear any answers that sounded even close to what he'd written. That wasn't a good sign.

All of a sudden, he had the overwhelming

sensation that he was a step behind. Like everyone else was running at a certain pace and he was the slow one, never able to catch up. He looked around at all the turtles in the room and nodded. "You guys get me," he said.

Mr. Turtell came into the classroom just as the bell was ringing. He held up the stack of tests in his hand, then started to pass them out. "No reason to make you wait. Some of you will be relieved by the grades you got . . . but some of you will not."

Mr. Turtell returned each test to its owner facedown, so students could choose not to show their neighbors if they didn't want to. But this also meant it was up to each kid to decide when to flip it over and see the grade.

Some part of Micah wanted to slip the test into his backpack without even looking at it, putting it off for later. But what good would that do? He'd eventually have to find out.

Might as well get it over with. He flipped over the top corner, where the red writing was.

Did he see what he thought he saw? No! That couldn't be!

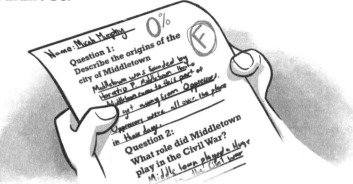

He looked at it again. At the top of the page was one big, painful letter, an F, along with an even more painful number: 0%.

He hadn't gotten anything right? At all? How was that possible? Didn't he get *some* credit—at least for the effort of writing stuff down? Apparently, not one thing he'd written even rose to the level of "sort of right," or "not quite, but almost." He couldn't have done worse if he'd doodled Captain Karate all over his paper.

Everyone was carefully reading over their tests, looking at the comments Mr. Turtell had left. But

to town, and I can go beg them for a job. No. That wouldn't work. He couldn't juggle, and he wasn't big enough to be the strong man, and he didn't have facial hair yet, so he couldn't be the bearded lady, and the smell of popcorn made him puke, so he couldn't sell circus snacks either . . .

Micah knew he was doing what his mom called "spiraling," letting his emotions overwhelm him until he couldn't think straight. But the thing about spiraling is, once you're doing it, it's hard to stop. You whirl around faster and faster, until you eventually get sucked down the toilet.

Somehow, he found himself already holding his red pen. He hadn't remembered taking it out of his desk, but it was in his hand, with the cap off.

Before he could think about it enough to stop himself, he drew a line. *The* line. The line on the right-hand side of the F, turning it into a misshapen A. And then, quick as he could, he added a 1, and then a 0, turning the 0% into 100%.

My Worst Decisions (up to this point)

- When I was seven, I cut my sister's hair with clippers while she was asleep. I wanted to pretend I had a big brother who was home from the Navy.

- When I was eight, I caught a fish on a camping trip and wanted to keep it for my aquarium. My mom wouldn't let me, so I hid it in her duffel bag, wrapped in a wet towel, thinking it would be okay until I got home. It was not.

- When I was nine, I biked to Gordo Burgers and ate three loaded cheeseburgers. Then I decided there is always room for a milkshake. Later, I met my friends at Pukey Pete's and rode the Super Twist-Master fourteen times. Ride number fourteen, it turned out, was a mistake.

- Earlier this year, I wanted to impress my friends with a tattoo of Captain Karate Dino Cop. When you're drawing on your shoulder, you have to draw upside down. And as it turns out, I'm not very good at that—which is something I probably should have thought about before I used a permanent marker. Captain Karate ended up looking like a manatee in a sundress. And it was picture day.

Just like that. It was done. There was no turning back.

That's when he suddenly realized . . . this may have been the worst decision he'd ever made.

Time seemed to stand still. Eventually Micah could hear voices around him.

"Earth to Micah," Armin said. "I asked you what you got."

"I . . . uh . . . ," stammered Micah.

He flipped the paper over.

"100%?" Armin whispered. "How is that possible?"

Lydia leaned over Micah's desk, so no one else could hear her other than Armin and Micah. "It's not! Walter Tisdale didn't even get a 100%, and he's the history expert on my Quiz Bowl team! There's no way you got a 100%!"

"You don't know that! I could've!" Micah said.

Lydia picked up the paper. "Seriously?

You wrote:

"'Middletown was founded by Horatio P. Middletown. Horatio Middletown came to this part of the country to get away from Oppressors. Oppressors were all over the place in those days. They were always telling people what to do. It was awful. Horatio Middletown just wanted to be left alone and make his living as a weasel trapper. Weasels were big business back then. They were small and skinny, so people would train them to get into tight spaces, such as squeezing between seat cushions on their covered wagons to find loose change. That sort of thing. Soon the area attracted weasel trappers from the East Coast who were fed up with the Weasel Tax Act of 1752. Middletown grew and grew.'"

"Really, Micah?" Armin asked. "Weasels?"

"Weasel trapping was huge back then," Micah whispered. "You must've missed that in Mr. Turtell's lecture."

"Let me see that test," Armin said. "Question 2: What role did Middletown play in the Civil War?

You wrote:

> "'Middletown played a huge role in the Civil War! No one was more civil than Middletown. Everyone always said please and thank you and called people sir and ma'am." Eventually, the bad guys had to give up. The Civil War was won!'"

"What was wrong with that one?" Micah huffed.

Lydia just rolled her eyes and grabbed the paper back from Armin. "Question 3: Describe a leading industry in Middletown today. You wrote:

> "'SmoothieTown is, of course, one of the biggest industries in Middletown. They manufacture smoothies there. They're awesome. The most popular is mango banana, but I prefer the ones that aren't on the menu, like orange slime, which is a blend of peaches, yams, and ranch dressing. Pig Slop, made with strawberries, sundried tomatoes, Oreo cookies, and barbecue sauce, is another nice blend. People in Middletown see big things for SmoothieTown in the future. I heard a rumor they are going to open up another store on 35th and Monroe. Maybe I'll get to work there someday.'"

"I can't believe you wrote about SmoothieTown!" Armin said.

"Of course I did," Micah said. "I read an article about them in *Middletown Business Monthly*. They're a huge industry!" Micah hated himself for piling one lie on top of another like this. But now he couldn't stop himself.

"I got a C+!" Micah heard Gabe say to no one in particular. "It's my best grade so far this year!"

Micah put his head in his hands. He'd reached a new low.

"Tell us the truth, Micah," Lydia whispered. "What happened?"

"Just because you didn't know the stuff I wrote on my test doesn't mean it wasn't all true! Look at the top of the test. I got a 100%! Mr. Turtell must have thought my answers were great."

"Micah," Armin said, "we know you. We also know Mr. Turtell. Something funny is going on here. Why are you lying to us?"

Micah sighed. He realized he wouldn't be able

to fool his best friends. He leaned even closer to Lydia and Armin so absolutely no one else could hear. "Fine. I changed my grade from an F to an A. I just couldn't stand the thought of failing that big."

"I wonder if my mom will frame my test!" Gabe thought out loud.

"There's no way you'll ever get away with it," Lydia whispered to Micah.

"And besides," Armin added, "it's one thing to lie on the test. But I can't believe you lied to us!"

"She'll definitely write about my grade in the Christmas letter!" Gabe exclaimed.

"I'm sorry, guys," Micah apologized. "But please don't tell anyone."

"Fine. We won't," Lydia said. "But we also won't lie if anyone asks."

"That's fair," Micah whispered.

"No, actually it's not," corrected Armin. "You owe us big."

"Well, it probably won't matter anyway. I

think I'll just throw away my test and never show anyone."

"What are we whispering about?" Gabe asked, trying to see over Lydia's shoulder. "I love whispering! Whispering's the best!"

He stretched over Lydia to see Micah's test. "Hey, everybody! Micah got a 100%! Good job, Micah!"

Micah sighed and shook his head.

"Huh!" said Mr. Turtell. "I don't remember you getting such a good grade, Micah."

"I . . . er . . . ," Micah stammered.

"Let me see that." Mr. Turtell came around to Micah's desk and looked at the paper. "The red ink never lies! You did get a 100%."

Is he kidding me right now? Micah wondered. *How long will it take before he recognizes his mistake?*

But Mr. Turtell just went on. "Congratulations, young man. An A! Who would've thought it was possible?"

"Not me," Lydia muttered under her breath.

"I knew you could do it!" said Gabe.

All through the rest of class, Micah had a queasy feeling in his stomach, like he'd just eaten a food-truck tamale. He couldn't stop thinking about all the lies and wondered what it would lead to. Yep, it was definitely better to be a failure than a liar. What had he been thinking?

The bell rang, and everyone lined up to go to the lunchroom. Chet snuck up behind Micah and grabbed him by the waist of his pants. Before Micah could brace himself, Chet yanked him up in the air, giving him his daily wedgie.

But then, to Micah's surprise, before Chet released him, he gave his pants an upward twist, making things particularly uncomfortable.

"That last move was new," Armin said, once Chet had finally let go of Micah.

"Yeah," Chet said. "He used to just be a geek. Now he's a nerd too, so I felt like I had to step it up a notch."

Lydia nodded. "Makes sense to me."

The Big F

I'm no straight-A student, but an F?! I didn't know I was capable of getting a zero on a test! Yep, I got an F on my history test. What's worse, I told a HUGE lie. I've reached an all-time low.

I should have just owned up to the fact that I didn't study. Now I've really messed up! I made everyone believe I'm some kind of genius by changing my test grade. Why didn't I change it to something believable? How am I going to keep up this façade?

Tell the truth, the whole truth, when you speak.
Zechariah 8:16 (MSG)

▷ **What do YOU think will happen if Micah keeps up his lie?**

▷ **What would YOU do if you got a really bad grade on a test?**

CHAPTER FOUR

"Hi, Micah! How did you do on your test?"

Really? This was the first thing his mom had to say as soon as he walked through the door? Not even a warm-up question, like, "How was your day?"

"What test?" Micah asked, trying to buy time so he could figure a way out of lying to his parents.

"Your big history test, of course! How did you do on it?"

"Um . . . fine, I guess."

"What does that mean?" his dad asked. "Give us some specifics. A letter, perhaps? Or maybe a number? You know how grades work, don't you, kiddo?"

"I . . . got an A," Micah answered quietly, hanging his backpack on the hook on the wall.

"Micah got an A!" cheered his mom.

"Micah got an A!" cheered his dad.

"Micah got an A?" asked his sister.

"That's terrific, Micah," his dad said. "How many questions did you miss?"

Micah didn't want to lie again, but at this point there was no turning back. "None," he said sheepishly.

His mom stared at him in shock, then dabbed the corners of her eyes with a tissue.

His dad grinned from ear to ear. "My boy's a genius! Who would've thought?"

"Not me," Audrey said. She glared at Micah suspiciously from the sofa, then shook her head and went back to reading book 1 of the Amish Vampire Chronicles.

Micah's dad put an arm around his shoulder. "Micah, this opens up a world of possibilities for you!"

"You could be a history teacher!" suggested his mom.

"A history *professor*!" added his dad.

"An archaeologist!" said his mom.

"A con man," sniped Audrey.

"A politician!" said his dad.

"Same thing," said Audrey.

"The president!" said his mom.

They stood there in silence, each imagining a country where Micah was in charge. Micah wore a look of dignified confidence; his mom and dad, looks of pride; his sister, a look of horrified disbelief.

"Micah, your mom and I were going to talk to you about something later, but now seems as good a time as any to bring it up."

His mom smiled. "We were thinking about letting you go to Pukey Pete's CoasterTown Amusement Park for their Fall Finale weekend! You'll have to get a C average on your report card, but now that seems like a sure thing! You can get Cs in your sleep!"

Micah hesitated. "I don't think I really deserve that. It was just one test."

"Nonsense!" his dad said. "You worked really hard studying for it!"

Micah shrugged. "Okay, then. That would be great. Armin, Lydia, and Gabe are all going too!"

"Well, you earned it, Micah!" His dad gave him a pat on the back. "We're all very proud of you."

"Do you have your test with you?" his mom asked. "I'd love to see it."

This was another question Micah had hoped to avoid. But he supposed there was no way around it.

He pulled the test out of his backpack and handed it to his mom.

With his dad looking over her shoulder, she looked at the grade at the top of the page and smiled. Then they both sat down at the kitchen table and read the whole test cover to cover, as if it were a brand-new novel from their favorite author. At last they put it down. "Fascinating! Absolutely fascinating!" said his mom. "I learned so much! Some of these crazy stories are just unbelievable!"

"I couldn't agree more," said Audrey, not even bothering to look up from her book this time.

Life as a fraud. It wasn't going to be easy. Especially as an up-and-coming vlogger. It was ironic that one of the reasons Micah had wanted to change his grade was because of his vlog, but now that he'd changed it, it was one of the worst parts of his lie. After all, his vlog had become the one place where he could really open up and be honest with the world, letting people in on all the highs and lows of life in fifth grade. No pretty picture, of course, but at least it was real. And that's what his seven—no, eight—fans had come to expect.

Now, being honest about his test or how smart he isn't might get back to the people that mattered. What if his mom watched his vlog! Micah thought she at least clicked on it briefly to give him an official "view," and every once in a while, even a "like." (Being willing to give a "like" was a big deal for her—she didn't give them out to just anyone!)

But now his online world of creating honest art for the masses had been tainted! He didn't want his vlog posts to be just another part of his great big lie, so he'd continue being honest, and if someone found out the truth, then at least life could go back to normal.

The next day, in the lunchroom, Micah pushed his cream of zucchini casserole around his plate. It smelled like something a humpback whale might cough up after eating old tuna. Still, Micah had a feeling the disgusting casserole thought it was too good for him. Maybe it was right.

Armin and Lydia sat down beside Micah and stared at their own plates. It was that kind of meal.

Armin tapped the casserole with his fork and watched it jiggle. "Are we sure this is food?"

"The results haven't come back from Mr. Beaker's lab yet," Lydia said.

Armin stopped prodding his meal and turned to Micah. "You've had quite a week."

New Leaf Elementary School
Casserole Recipe

It's easy to re-create your favorite school lunch casserole at home. Just follow these simple steps:

Step 1: Gather vegetables, spices, and sauces from back of pantry. Don't be particular about which ones. Keep an eye out for ingredients that happen to be growing other ingredients on top of them. These "bonus ingredients" can add surprising flavors to your meal!

Step 2: Mix together in a bowl until you can't tell one ingredient from another. Words like "sludge," "slime," and "ooze" should come to mind. If they don't, keep mixing.

Step 3: Add food coloring until your sludge turns brown. Then pour into a baking dish.

Step 4: Ask your mom if you can borrow her oven, and then bake the casserole at, like, 500 degrees (or whatever) until your mom yells, "What's burning?"

Step 5: Check your casserole. If the mixture looks congealed and you can poke it with a fork without breaking the skin, it's ready to be served.

"Yeah, a little more attention than I'd like."

"Whose fault is that?" Lydia asked.

Micah sighed. He had a better chance impressing the casserole than ever impressing Lydia.

Out of nowhere, PB and J (New Leaf's student news crew) showed up with a camera and microphone. J pulled Micah up out of his seat and shoved the microphone in his face. "We're here with the ONLY kid in fifth grade who got a 100% on Mr. Turtell's big history test! Micah, how'd you get so smart?"

"Uh . . . studying, I guess."

"And how does it feel to be the smartest kid in school?" asked PB.

"I"—Micah looked over at Lydia and saw her glaring at him—"wouldn't know."

"Ha!" laughed PB. "He's humble, too! Almost too good to be true, this guy!"

"We love the humble ones, don't we, PB?"

"That's right, J! As long as we don't have to be humble ourselves!"

"You said it, PB!"

PB motioned to his cameraman, Will. "That's a wrap! Put it in the can for the 3:30 report."

And as quickly as they'd come, they disappeared.

"That was weird," Armin said.

Gabe came over to their table with a brown lunch bag. There was a note on it that said, *Enjoy your lunch, Gaberooni! Love, Mom.* Gabe looked over at Micah's plate. "Rats! I shouldn't have packed my lunch. I missed cream of zucchini casserole day again!"

Chet came up behind Micah and gave his shoulder a harder-than-necessary push. "Hey nerd, you think you're so smart? How about you help me study for the next test?"

"I thought you didn't like nerds," said Lydia.

Chet shrugged. "I use plenty of things I don't like. Just the other day I used math to count my stolen lunch money."

"Good point."

Suddenly Micah was surrounded by fifth graders.

"Micah, can you help me study too?" asked Abby.

"Me too!" said Akira.

"Hey, I was here first!" said Timothy.

"Okay, okay," Micah interrupted. "I'll let you all know. Maybe we can do a group study session or something."

He finally convinced them to go back to their seats. Micah looked over at Gabe, who was staring at him with a big grin on his face. "I would love it if you tutored me in history! Maybe I could get a B‑ next time! My mom says history is important so that I don't do stupid things other people have already done. She says, 'Always do your own stupid things, Gabe!'"

"That's good advice," Lydia said.

Gabe went on without missing a beat. "I love geography, especially Canada! My mom tells me not to love Canada so much, because it's unpatriotic to love other countries. But they have such great bacon!"

Micah was torn. He wanted to come clean with Gabe about his test, but he didn't think Gabe was very good at keeping secrets. When Gabe heard the Tooth Fairy might be make-believe, he spread it around the school's kindergarten classes so fast it would make your head spin. Which was odd, since he was in fourth grade at the time.

But Micah figured telling him was worth the risk. It would be good for Gabe to be in the know, along with Lydia and Armin. He started to explain it slowly. "Gabe, what would you think if I told you someone got a good grade on their history test even though they just made up all their answers?"

Gabe looked shocked. "You're not supposed to do that in history! You're only supposed to do that in math."

Maybe this was a bad idea. "Never mind."

"Okay," said Gabe. "You gonna eat your casserole?"

Fraud

I'm not sure what's worse . . . lying to my parents or lying to my friends? If Gabe really knew the truth, he wouldn't act so proud of me. I'm a fraud. How will I ever enjoy Pukey Pete's Fall Finale Weekend with this guilt weighing on me? I don't deserve a reward.

At least it's just the one lie. I can figure a way out of this. I guess I could pray and ask for God's help. But would He even be willing to help me after what I've done?

GOD is fair and just; He corrects the misdirected, sends them in the right direction. Psalm 25:8 (MSG)

> **What do YOU think Micah should do to make things right?**

> **Have YOU ever told a big lie? What happened?**

CHAPTER FIVE

The next day, Micah was walking down the fifth-grade hall, minding his own business, when out of nowhere Mr. Turtell popped out of a doorway up ahead. Micah felt a sudden desire to hide, but he was out in the open, with nothing to duck behind. Their eyes locked.

"Micah! Just who I was looking for. Do you have a moment?"

He didn't wait for Micah to respond.

"Micah, I'll be blunt. You're our only hope! We've got a Quiz Bowl match tonight after school, and Walter Tisdale is out with the mumps. Or was it the measles? I know it was one of those diseases I thought we'd gotten rid of years ago." Mr. Turtell didn't come up for air.

"Anyway, Walter was our history specialist. There's no one on the team who can even hold a candle to that boy when it comes to the past. Ha! Candle! That's a history thing. I'm hilarious! Anyway, with your mind for history, you're the perfect fill in!"

Micah had heard Lydia mention Quiz Bowl once or twice, but he didn't know much about it. But he figured she probably wouldn't be too happy if he joined the team. He needed to come up with a good excuse for getting out of this. "So, what exactly is a quiz bowl, anyway?" Micah asked.

"It's just like the Super Bowl, but better!" Micah had never seen Mr. Turtell so excited. "Instead of superstar athletes and millions of screaming fans, there are superstar students and ten to twelve parents who quietly cheer while being careful not to disturb the sanctity of the 'Quiz Chamber.'"

"That sounds . . . awesome?" Micah knew he

didn't sound very convincing. He also knew Mr. Turtell didn't even notice.

"Your friend Lydia is on the team! She's a whiz at math, as you probably know. But she's no history expert, like you."

Micah knew Lydia wasn't exactly thrilled with him right now. She would certainly not appreciate his "help," since he was confident he'd do more harm than good on the team.

"I don't think it's a good idea," Micah answered. "I'd be coming in after the season's already started and wouldn't know the rules."

"I'm sure Lydia would be glad to tell you everything you need to know about how the game is played!"

"I don't want her to have to do that."

Mr. Turtell put his arm on Micah's shoulder and looked him straight in the eye. "Micah, your school needs you! Will you rise to the challenge?"

Micah just couldn't think of anything to say. His lie about the test had gotten him into this mess, and now he had to deal with the consequences. "I . . . guess so."

"Not exactly the rousing words of Patrick Henry or William Wallace, but I suppose they'll do."

Two hours later, Micah found himself in a dimly lit music classroom that had been converted into a mini auditorium. Someone, likely Mr. Turtell, had placed a podium with some desks behind it at one end of the room, and a rolling platform with a dozen chairs on it at the other. (They weren't allowed to use the real auditorium because of auditions for Miss Petunia's upcoming musical, *What's at Steak?* He couldn't decide which place would be worse—there or here. After giving it some thought, he landed on "here." He felt a little sick to his stomach.)

Peppy game-show music was playing on a portable CD player. By this point, exactly eleven parents had wandered quietly into the room, filling up most of the chairs on the rolling platform, and were looking quietly at their phones or waving awkwardly at their sons and daughters. Other than parents, the only other fan in attendance was Gabe. Micah wasn't sure if he wanted a friend in the crowd to watch him embarrass himself or not, but in general it was hard to get embarrassed in front of Gabe.

The moderator was Mrs. Swanson, Micah's third-grade teacher, who he figured was probably around 112 years old by now.

Having her as moderator might not be ideal. She was no pushover and had never been particularly impressed with Micah's efforts. Which, he admitted, was fair.

Mrs. Swanson stood up from one of the chairs on the platform and made her way to the podium.

The first several questions were luckily not in Micah's area of "expertise," which was supposedly history. They were impossibly hard math problems, like taking the square root of poly-whatnots or English questions about diagramming sentences with plu-preposterous verb tenses in them. Did he even speak the same language as these nerds?

Surprising Math Fun Facts

A polygon is a shape made of many straight lines. Therefore, a bi-gon must be a shape made of only two straight lines. It is very hard to draw. In fact, it's so frustrating to draw, that when grown-ups want to forget about something bad that's happened, they sometimes use the expression, "Let bi-gons be bi-gons!"

According to mathematicians, if A is greater than B and B is greater than C, then A is greater than C. Which is why mathematicians are terrible at rock, paper, scissors.

You may have heard that the shortest distance between two points is a straight line. What fewer people know is that the longest distance between two points is also a straight line. But in the opposite direction.

In math, multiplying two negatives equals a positive. But that's not true with insults. For example, when Micah's sister, Audrey, makes fun of his shirt, she can't make him feel better by also making fun of his pants. But that doesn't keep her from trying.

Most of the Middletown team didn't seem to be understanding much better than he was. Lydia was doing well with the poly-whatnot stuff, but the others looked a bit lost.

Ten minutes into the competition, Mrs. Swanson announced the upcoming subject was history. Micah slowly walked up to the microphone. He could feel the sweat beading up on his forehead. Maybe he'd get lucky with the question. But Micah getting lucky didn't seem to be the trend these days.

Mrs. Swanson looked at him lazily, like a tiger sizing up a puny little rabbit hopping by, wondering if it was even worth the bother to eat.

"What is an assembly line, and who invented it?" she asked.

Micah wasn't sure he knew the answer, but at least she was using words he was familiar with. That was something. He stared up at the ceiling thoughtfully, pretending to think, like he'd seen other students do.

Let's see . . . what did he know about assemblies? He thought back to a few months ago when the school had an assembly. Fireman Bill had visited to talk to the kids about how, if there's a fire, you should "stop, drop, and roll." For some reason Gabe had decided to give it a try right there in the bleachers, rolling all the way down until he'd landed on the auditorium floor, thirty feet below. Everybody went crazy. Assemblies were awesome.

Micah thought about the whole assembly process and figured he had a reasonable answer. But based on the "reasonable answers" he'd put on his history test, he had absolutely no confidence he was right. How had he gotten himself into this mess again? His lie about his grade kept growing and growing. It was getting out of control.

He could feel his stomach churning as he leaned toward the microphone and started to speak. "An assembly line is . . ."

Uh-oh. He swallowed hard and took a deep breath.

He tried again. "An assembly line is . . ."

Suddenly, his stomach gave way. Up came his school lunch, all over the microphone and onto the floor.

Everyone stared at Micah in silence for a moment—until all the girls in the room yelled, "Ewwww!" like someone had held up a cue card.

"Excuse me," he said quietly. Then he headed for the exit. Behind him he heard Mrs. Swanson say, "Let's take a five-minute break for . . . uh

. . . tidying up. And then we'll get back to our questions."

After the match, Micah walked over to Lydia, who was talking to Gabe in the corner.

Gabe looked from Lydia to Micah. "Sorry about you getting sick. That happens to me every time I talk into a microphone!"

After Gabe walked away, Micah whispered to Lydia. "I know that was embarrassing, but probably not as embarrassing as if I'd actually tried to answer the questions."

Lydia smiled. "And it was definitely less harmful to our chances of winning."

"No doubt," Micah agreed.

"Still, I was sorry to see you get sick like that in front of everyone. It's hard to sit there and watch your friend embarrass himself." Micah thought he caught a hint of a smile on Lydia's face. "Although I should be used to it by now," she added.

Quiz Bowl

How in the world did one "good grade" land me in the Quiz Bowl?! Imagine: Micah Murphy in an academic challenge with the school's best brainiacs . . . What a joke! Mr. Turtell asked me to join the team, and since I'm the new "genius" in class, I just had to roll with it. Is he *ever* going to realize that he posted the wrong grade?

Thankfully, I managed to get out of trying to answer any questions. I had to puke all over the microphone, but it was worth it. All in all, the experience was only mildly embarrassing. I don't think things could get any worse. I'd better figure out how to get out of this lie before it does . . .

Give all your worries and cares to God, for he cares about you.
1 Peter 5:7 (NLT)

▷ **Would YOU rather be exposed for lying, or puke in front of your classmates?**

▷ **What do YOU think Micah should do next?**

CHAPTER SIX

Dogs are the best. You can be completely honest with them about anything and everything, and they never judge you. On the other hand, maybe dogs are just really good actors, secretly judging you all the time as they wag their tails and lick you in the face. Who knows?

Either way, dogs are a great comfort for boys with a guilty conscience, and Micah was excited to get home and hang out with his mutt, Barnabas.

Moms, on the other hand, are terrible for boys with a guilty conscience. They're always asking awkward questions about things you don't want to talk about. Ever since Micah lied about his history test, he would come home from school every day and play a round of dodge-the-mom as he looked for Barnabas so he could take him on a walk. Today his dodging game was off.

He'd walked around the back of his house and come in the basement door. Unfortunately, his mom was just taking laundry out of the dryer. Barnabas rushed down the stairs with the leash in his mouth, but couldn't get there in time to cut off Micah's mom before she greeted him with a hug.

"There's my little genius!"

"Hardly," he said.

She ignored him. "I just heard about an amazing opportunity! Do you remember Mr. Leafblatt, the town historian?"

"Is he your old friend with the big ears?"

"They're actually normal-sized. His tiny head just makes them look big."

"Oh."

"He gives tours of Old Middletown every night."

Micah rubbed Barnabas's head. "Middletown has tourists?"

"Of course we do! And Mr. Leafblatt gets to show them around all the amazing historic sites. Or at least he used to. Sadly, he's going to have to take some time off. He twisted his ankle on a dead possum. He didn't even see it lying there when he was walking backwards leading the tour."

"It might not have really been dead," Micah said. "They fake it sometimes, you know."

"Oh, this one was dead, all right. Ruined his shoes."

"Ew."

"The point is, you'd be a perfect replacement! You know all about local history. And you'll probably make a little tip money too!"

Micah shook his head. "I really don't think that's a good idea. I'm just a kid! Won't the tourists be expecting a grown-up expert?"

"I think you'd be awesome! My friends at the historic society thought they were going to have to shut down their tours, but when I told them you'd do it, everyone was just tickled pink!"

"But I . . ."

His mom held his face in her hands and looked him in the eye. "Micah, your town needs you!"

Where had he heard that before?

How had one lie about a grade on a test led to this? But what was he supposed to do now? At this point he couldn't possibly tell his mom he was really no good at history.

He sighed. "I guess so."

"Excellent! You'll be wonderful. Now we just have to find some hose and a wig that fits you."

"Did you say hose and a wig?"

"Of course I did! It's a history tour, and you have to look historically accurate! Everyone in colonial times wore hose and wigs—Washington, Adams, Jefferson."

"But you don't even make Audrey wear that stuff, and she's a girl!"

"If it's good enough for George Washington and Thomas Jefferson, it's good enough for you!"

Things That Would Be Less Embarrassing Than Wearing Hose and a Wig Around Town

1. Mom shouting, "Goodbye! I love you, little man!" at school drop-off

2. Dad telling one of his corny jokes to my friends (unfortunately, this one happens all the time)

3. Being tutored in math by a 3rd grader

4. My friends finding out I'm being tutored by a 3rd grader

5. Wearing one of Ms. Petunia's vegetable costumes

6. Arriving at school before realizing Audrey put my favorite teddy bear in my backpack

7. Puking in front of my classmates (oh wait—I just did that)

8. Showing up at school with a big hole in the back of my pants

9. Forgetting to put on my pants (this one may or may not have happened once)

"But George Washington and Thomas Jefferson didn't have to face Chet and Hanz at New Leaf Elementary the next day."

"Don't worry. You'll look adorable!"

Micah hated to have to talk to his mom like this, but he had to put his foot down. "I'm telling you right now, there's no way I'll ever be caught dead in hose and a wig!"

Walking down Main Street the next day, Micah caught his reflection in a store window and sighed. He looked ridiculous in the wig his mom had insisted he wear, although he had to admit the hose were surprisingly comfortable. At least he'd be ready to sign any declarations that happened to come his way.

He headed for Town Hall, a big, columned building with peeling paint and a bored attitude—if it had a choice, it would probably get up and go someplace more interesting. The only somewhat interesting thing to see in the whole town square was a horse-drawn carriage slowly ambling by. The old couple inside the carriage looked as if they were having the time of their lives. Micah suddenly wished he were old, because by then maybe he would stop getting himself into all these ridiculous messes.

In front of the building there was a sign that read, "Historic Middletown tours start here!" Micah hoped no one would actually show up—or at least not very many—but to his surprise, seventeen people were already lined up. What was he going to say to all these people? The town had blown off his request for training. "You're a boy genius," they declared. "You'll figure it out."

Micah walked to the front of the crowd. "This is the town hall," he began.

His voice sounded small and squeaky. He tried to speak louder, hoping it would clear up. "Um . . . it's where they have a bunch of meetings about the town. The mayor is there sometimes, I think. It's a pretty old building."

He was losing the crowd, and he knew it. Maybe now was the time to run away.

"When was it built?" asked a man in front. He had a fanny pack and was drinking out of a Big Sipper soda cup.

"1806." The year came out without Micah even thinking about it. Why couldn't he just admit it when he didn't know stuff?

The Big Sipper man nodded, accepting Micah's made-up fact. Which was kind of fun.

"The town hall was very important during the Civil War," Micah said. "The Union army used it as a hospital, so it was pretty rough in there. People were always getting stuff amputated. Legs. Arms. Ears. Noses. If it stuck out, they'd cut it off."

"Was that because of gangrene?" asked an older woman in the back.

"Um . . . yeah. Gang green. Gang yellow. All the gangs were big back then."

Micah glanced at the map the historical society had given him and started walking toward the next site before anyone could ask any more questions. They all walked down the cobblestone road toward the Second Street bridge. "The brick they made this road out of was mined in Latin America by baboons. They're great workers if you treat them well. Just don't get on their bad side. A baboon revolt can be deadly."

"I thought baboons were from Africa," said a third grader. Micah thought he recognized him from school.

"Er . . . of course they are, but there was a lot of monkey trading back in the 1800s—baboons for . . . uh . . . South American monkeys. It was big business."

The boy looked skeptical. "That doesn't sound right."

His mother gave him a stern look. "I'm sure he

knows more about the history of this town than you do. He's wearing a colonial wig, after all!"

Micah moved on as quickly as he could. "And this bridge was also built in the early 1800s. If you remember from your history lessons, colonial rebels threw a hundred gallons of tropical punch off this bridge to protest English punch taxes."

Thoughtful looks passed over the faces in the crowd as everyone tried to remember back to their old history classes.

"There was tropical punch back then?" a young woman asked.

"It was rare," another man answered. "That's why throwing it in the river was such a big deal. That punch must've been worth a fortune!"

Micah didn't expect help from the crowd, but rolled with it. "Absolutely! It cost hundreds of dollars! Which is, like, worth a lot more today."

A tall, thin man in the back shook his fist. "Those dadburn tropical punch companies are still sticking it to the little guy!"

"Don't get me started on the tropical punch cartel! They control everything!" Micah wasn't even sure what he was saying. He'd heard the word "cartel" before, and it sounded scary. He figured he'd better keep the tour moving along.

"And over here we have an old factory that used to make those triangle hats for people back in the old days."

"Why didn't they just wear round hats, like normal people?" asked the young woman.

Micah barely paused before an answer came to him. "If your triangle hat blows off on a windy day, it won't roll down the street as easily as a round hat."

He was really in the flow now! He almost felt as if some of the stuff he was saying was true. Maybe it was. He saw people in the crowd nodding their heads and one or two taking notes.

"And over here, there is more to this historic water tower than meets the eye. It has secret doors and panels. Back in the 1950s it was a missile launcher. The government used to disguise missile launchers as water towers so the Russians wouldn't know where they were."

He could hear several "oohs" and "ahs" from the crowd. One man said to a woman next to him, "I've suspected that for years!"

The rest of the tour was an exciting blur, and before he knew it, Micah had finished the loop and gotten back around to Town Hall. Everyone thanked him for such a surprising and fascinating tour, and some of them even gave him tips!

As the crowd walked away, he overheard a man say, "Finally, someone's willing to tell us the unvarnished truth about this town!"

The woman beside him said, "Yeah. I wonder how long it'll be before they shut this whistle-blower down!"

Micah had no idea what they meant, so he ignored them and counted his tips. Fourteen bucks! What a day!

TOO LATE

So much for figuring a way out before things got worse. Because I'm such a "local history buff," my mom signed me up to fill in for the town's tour guide. I just spent the afternoon completely making up stories about Middletown.

I wish I could stop all this lying, but I end up having to cover up every lie with more lies . . . it just keeps going–building up like a snowball! I can't help but feel this won't end well . . .

There is nothing hidden that will not be revealed. There is nothing kept secret that will not come to light.
Luke 8:17 (GW)

▷ **What could Micah have done when his mom asked him to be the tour guide?**

▷ **Why do YOU think one little lie often leads to bigger lies?**

CHAPTER SEVEN

It was Friday, and Micah was on his fourth day of being an Old Middletown tour guide, and with every tour the crowds grew bigger and bigger. But so did the lies. They were weighing on him more and more, and he was having trouble keeping them all straight. And he figured if he forgot his own lies and started contradicting himself, it would all quickly blow up in his face.

How did one little lie about a history test turn into such a big mess? Maybe there really weren't any "little" lies. Once you let yourself start lying, you never know how bad it's going to get.

Luckily there were only a few tours left before he was off the hook. He was ready to forget all about this weird little detour in his life.

But then the unthinkable happened.

After school he'd pulled up his hose, adjusted his wig, and rushed out the door, just as he'd been doing all week. All seemed right with the world. Or, if not quite right, then at least tolerable.

But as he was walking down Seventh Avenue on his way downtown, he spotted a familiar strut heading down a side street. Chet! Maybe he hadn't seen him.

Chet stopped. He stared. Even from fifty yards away, Micah could see Chet's eyes move up and down Micah's body, taking in the hose, the knee-high trousers, the men's blouse, the wig. The only question was whether or not he recognized the boy inside the costume.

"Ha! Micah, you look like my mom!"

Micah had a decision to make. He could do the smart thing: act like he hadn't heard him and walk as quickly as he could downtown. Or, he could talk back.

He was a little out of practice when it came to making smart decisions.

"So, are you saying your mom looks like a ten-year-old boy in a wig? She must be hideous!"

Micah watched Chet's eyes narrow. "That's it! I'm about to give you a wedgie so hard your pantyhose will split right in half."

"But they're my only pair!"

"And then I'm going to use your wig to mop up"—Chet paused as he tried to think up the grossest thing possible—"the bathrooms in the kindergarten wing!"

Micah couldn't believe his ears. "Nooooooo!"

Was Chet serious? Micah watched Chet's hands close into fists and his jaw clench in rage. In a sudden burst of speed, Chet shot down the road after him.

The chase was on!

Micah took off as fast as he could down Seventh. He figured the best thing he could do was head for the tour and hope a police officer happened to be somewhere nearby to keep Chet from carrying out his threats. Micah was already a full block ahead of him, which would have been enough under normal conditions. But colonial shoes, it turns out, are not ideal in a footrace.

Micah glanced behind him and saw how quickly Chet had shrunk the lead to half a block. He had to try something else. He quickly darted onto Poplar Street, turned left down an alley, then caught his breath behind a garbage can. He heard Chet follow down Poplar, but he missed Micah's turn down the alley and kept going straight.

As fast as he could, Micah doubled back the way he'd come, knowing Chet wouldn't be fooled for long.

He was just turning onto Seventh again when he saw something perfect. On the other side of Poplar, just outside the office of Olden Days Carriage Rides, stood a beautiful, gray horse, swishing his tail without a care in the world. What dumb luck!

Micah pictured himself galloping away, making a fast getaway from Chet, followed by a big, exciting entrance at Town Hall for the tour. The crowd would go crazy! Just imagine the tips he'd get!

He paused for a moment to think. Horse thieving was no small crime. He could be whipped or hanged! No—he was thinking like a colonial guy again. They probably didn't do that sort of thing anymore.

Besides, once he told the horse's owner he was just trying to get away from a bully named Chet, he'd surely understand.

The horse was perfectly positioned right beside a few wooden boxes. Micah hurried over to them and climbed up. He was now at the level of the horse's back. This was it! He'd never been on a horse before, but judging from what he'd seen in the movies, it was easy and it looked awesome! And he was certainly dressed for the occasion.

He swung one leg around and sat down.

Not bad. He was sure he looked amazing, like some Revolutionary War leader ready to attack . . . somebody or other. Which empire did the colonists fight again? The Romans? The Mongolians? Who cares? Right now he just had to get this thing going.

"Go," Micah said to the horse. Nothing.

"Seriously, I gotta be somewhere."

Still nothing.

Micah wondered if a ten-year-old boy in hose and a wig was just not intimidating enough to get a horse moving. But then his eye caught something he hadn't noticed before. A rope. Rats.

The horse was tied to the railing of the stairs. Micah hit himself on the forehead. Of course it was. If you happened to own an animal that is perfect for fast getaways, you're probably going to tie it up.

Micah got back off the horse so he could untie the rope.

As he started to pull at the knot, he glanced down Poplar. At the far end he could see Chet doubling back. Micah didn't think Chet had seen him just yet, since he was huddled between the horse and the platform, but if he kept coming this way, he'd see him soon enough. And Micah didn't know if he'd have enough time to untie the rope, jump on the horse, and figure out how to get it started.

Micah fiddled with the knot. Just as it was finally coming loose, he looked up to see Chet closing in on him.

"I'm a dead man," Micah whispered. Maybe if the horse heard him, he'd help Micah out of this jam. But it was too late. Micah dropped the rope at the sight of Chet's feet directly in front of him. He looked up slowly with a wince, preparing for the punch.

Just then, Chet yelled, "Ewwwww!!!!" and Micah realized the horse actually *had* come to his aid. Micah had been so freaked out when he saw Chet's shoes, he didn't realize his enemy had stepped in horse poop.

This was Micah's chance. "Sorry about your shoes!" he said with a grin as he took off running toward the town hall.

Micah hadn't gone far when he glanced back over his shoulder and saw Chet quickly scraping the poop off his shoes. Chet had seen Micah dart down Seventh Avenue. Now he took off after Micah.

Micah knew Chet was not about to let him get away, not now! By this time Micah was getting used to running in his old-timey buckle shoes, but Chet still had the advantage. Luckily for Micah, he'd gotten a head start.

Micah pushed himself as hard as his legs would go, but he wasn't sure it would be enough. He was two blocks away from Town Hall, and Chet was not far behind him.

Micah could hear Chet's heavy breathing grow closer and closer. He looked back and saw Chet's big, beefy hand reaching out, only inches away, to grab his collar and pull him down to the ground.

This was it. He was about to go down.

Then, suddenly, he heard shouting from just ahead.

"Don't chase our guide!"

"Yeah, leave him alone!"

Micah stopped.

Chet stopped.

On the lawn outside Town Hall was the biggest tour crowd yet.

"You're nothing but a bully!" a young woman shouted at Chet.

Chet started to explain. "But he said that my mom—"

"You're no better than the British!" an older man joined in. "Trying to keep us little guys down!"

"Yeah! No taxation without representation!" yelled an old woman.

Chet started to back away. "But I don't even know what that means!"

"Look it up, bully!" the young woman said.

Chet turned around and walked back the way he'd come. The crowd went crazy. Everybody loves a revolution.

There must have been a hundred people waiting for the tour! Micah's lies were spreading, and apparently people were believing them. He looked over the crowd, in shock that it was so huge. There were some unusual people there, including several men in black suits and shades. Huh. They must have come straight from work.

And was that Gabe? What was he wearing? And he wasn't the only one! There were about a dozen of them, all decked in colonial clothes, just like Micah's—the wigs, the tights, the knee-length pants, the buckled shoes. Micah recognized a couple of the younger kids from school, but there were also grown men and women wearing this stuff.

"What are you guys doing?" Micah asked.

A man Micah recognized from the grocery store answered. "We like your look."

"But it's not my *look*," Micah said. "It's a costume."

The man shrugged. "Whatever."

As Micah continued to scan the crowd, to his dismay he came across two other familiar faces: Lydia and Armin! His one comfort had been that he'd given the tours to a bunch of strangers who would quickly forget about him the moment it was over. No such luck this time.

Micah walked up to them. "I'm surprised to see you two here."

"We heard on the radio about a boy genius

giving history tours," Armin said. "We figured it was you, so we thought we'd come by to keep you from embarrassing yourself."

Lydia looked him up and down. "I think we're too late."

"Seriously, Micah," Armin said. "You can't keep this up."

"But my mom begged me to do it! She said the whole town was counting on me. So far it's gone pretty well. The people are loving the history I'm telling."

"Did you even do any research?" Lydia looked at his empty hands. "Don't answer that."

"The History Society didn't think I'd need any! I'm a boy genius with a gift for local history, remember?"

"Listen," said Lydia. "You've got to just tell everyone you quit and go home."

"But I already bought the tour map!" Gabe said.

Micah looked at Armin for help and sympathy.

"If you insist on keeping this up, you better get

going," Armin told him. "Your tour was supposed to start five minutes ago."

Micah nodded and headed back toward the crowd.

Micah held up his hand to get everyone's attention. With this huge crowd, he really was feeling stage fright, so maybe Lydia was right. But it would be so humiliating to quit now.

But once Micah got going, everyone went nuts for him every step of the way, and Micah couldn't help but follow their lead. Everything was bigger than ever. Rather than just a single Cold War missile in the water tower, all of a sudden, missiles were everywhere and Middletown had become the central line of defense against the entire Soviet Empire. And strange words started coming out of his mouth. He told a story about how in the roaring twenties— whatever they were—Mayor McGillicutty had ties to the Effluvian Empire. He mentioned something about a redacted manila envelope, and he didn't even know what the word "redacted" meant. And now that old triangle hat factory he'd mentioned a few tours ago had somehow slowly evolved into an enormous research lab that was attempting to use bubble wrap technology to create the world's first force field.

The crowd ate it up!

By the time the tour was over, the skies were darkening with rain clouds, but Micah was on top of the world. He'd never felt so appreciated!

Armin, Lydia, and Gabe came up to him.

"Can you believe it?" Micah asked. "I didn't embarrass myself!"

"Although you may have embarrassed your town," said Armin.

Lydia shook her head at Micah. "I can't believe you just made up all that stuff!"

"Just because you didn't know about it, doesn't mean it's all made-up," Gabe said.

"But . . ." Lydia threw her hands in the air. "Never mind."

"How long are you going to keep this up?" Armin asked.

"Just a few tours more," said Micah. "My mom's counting on me! The town is counting on me! I've got to keep going!"

"You've got to be kidding! I'm out of here." Lydia glared at Micah one last time, then stomped away. Gabe followed her.

"I agree with Lydia," added Armin. "I think you should tell your mom the truth. And the town would be better off without any more of your tours anyway."

They were both right, of course. One lie had led to another and another. But it was just so hard to stop! There were too many people it would disappoint. And if he admitted his lies now, everyone would know how dumb he really was. He just couldn't do it.

As Micah continued to gather all his tips, Armin whispered in his ear. "Did you happen to see those men in black suits?"

He had. Micah glanced in their direction. Sure enough, it was the same men Micah had seen earlier. But this time Micah noticed that in addition to the dark glasses, they also had black ear buds and wires, and they were staring back at him.

"I'm sure it's nothing."

"Micah," said Armin, "they look serious. And official, if you know what I mean."

Neither boy had noticed that Gabe had returned while they were talking. "You mean like librarians?" he asked, making both Micah and Armin jump.

"No, like government spooks," Armin answered. "CIA. NSA. FBI."

"Whatever you're trying to spell, I don't think you're spelling it right," said Gabe. "Cian Safbi doesn't mean anything."

Armin rolled his eyes. "You've heard of the CIA, right? And the NSA and the FBI? Micah, I think they're onto you! You can't just go around making up history and expect to get away with it. People care about the past around here!"

"Really?" Micah asked. "In Middletown? I'm sure these guys are just tourists like everybody else."

But Micah wasn't really sure. There was a small part of him that thought Armin might be onto something. Still, he couldn't stop now. Things were going too well. "Either way, I will not be silenced! Isn't freedom of speech what our forefathers fought for?"

"Yes, but I don't know about this, Micah. Lies always come back to haunt you one way or another."

But Micah didn't have time to give it serious thought. Suddenly he was surrounded by cameras and microphones. He saw PB and J trying to push their way through a crowd of news reporters from local newspapers and networks. To Micah's surprise, they were a welcome sight among all the strange faces and intimidating equipment.

But just as PB and J were about to get to the front of the crowd, the smiling face of news correspondent Stormy McAllister pushed in front of them. "I'm here with local boy genius and tour guide, Micah Murphy. He's the biggest thing to hit this town since . . . muskrat trapping and orange slime smoothies! Micah, tell us how you know so much about Middletown!"

"I j-just . . . ," Micah stammered, "read a lot and pay attention."

"Such wise words from someone so young!" Stormy said. As the camera panned off Micah, he glanced back to where the men in black suits had been standing. They were gone. He searched for them through the still-gathered crowd, but they seemed to have vanished entirely. A shudder passed through him. Meanwhile, the clouds continued to darken the skies.

Stormy now had the microphone in the face of

a middle-aged man in dark-rimmed glasses. "Let's turn to the mayor of this fine town to get a few words. Mayor Kim, you must be tickled pink that our town has suddenly taken to history!"

"Actually, I have no idea what all the fuss is about. It doesn't make any sense."

"We're all glad to have a local kid hero getting our town excited about its roots!"

"But he's just making stuff up!"

"Are you saying he's a conspiracy theorist, basing his facts on rumors and unsubstantiated claims?"

"No. I don't think he's basing his facts on anything at all, substantiated or not. I think he's just making stuff up. It's all ridiculous, and I won't stand for it! He's slandering the good name of this town and its leadership. Mayor McGillicutty, for example, was an upstanding man and had absolutely no ties to the Effluvian Empire! And where on earth did this boy get that ridiculous information about the redacted manila envelope?!"

Stormy laughed lightly and looked into the camera. "Sounds like someone is a little jealous of all the attention Mr. Murphy is getting. Back to you in the studio, James!"

But apparently the media wasn't done with Micah just yet!

PB and J were now at the front of the crowd. "Can you give us a few minutes of your time for the students at New Leaf?" PB asked.

Micah was about to say yes when a woman from the *Middletown Daily* interrupted. "Micah, could we get a few shots of you for tomorrow's paper?" A dozen or so other newspaper reporters were standing around her with notebooks and cameras.

"If we play it right, I think this story could go national!" said one of the cameramen.

Micah adjusted his wig and tried to look historical.

A woman shook her head. "Something's not working."

Other Top Local News Stories of the Year
• Two of the sixteen downtown square blocks now free of rotten cantaloupe smell
• Local man finds missing car keys in back pocket . . . thought they were in front pocket
• Middletown declared ninth best midsized city in America for raising free-range dwarf llamas
• Ancient Indian burial mounds may be interrupting your cell phone reception
• Scientists say influx of out-of-town squirrels messing with local ecology
OPEN
NO ROTTEN CANTALOUPE smell!

Another reporter nodded. "We need to think bigger."

"Could you move up the Town Hall steps, so you look more official?"

Micah moved up the steps and gave them his smartest, most colonial look.

"Still not quite right. You don't happen to have one of those feather pens, do you?"

"Or a musket?"

Micah checked his pockets just in case, then shook his head.

The reporter sighed. "If only we had a horse."

"Actually," Micah said. "I think there may be a guy who gives carriage rides just down the street."

"That's it! That's just what we need for a big splash!"

It only took a few minutes for a couple of reporters to come back with a horse—the very horse Micah had tried to use to escape Chet. Well, he hadn't gotten his fast getaway and big entrance, but at least he'd still look great in the local paper tomorrow! Maybe even national ones!

One of the reporters helped Micah into the saddle, and everyone started taking pictures. He'd never felt so important! So popular! So impressive! So historical!

All of a sudden, rain started falling. Hard. Not just with a few small drops, but all at once, like someone dumping spaghetti water into the sink. Everyone started fleeing for shelter, which Micah—still on horseback—was unfortunately unable to do.

"PB and J? A little help here?" Micah called out.

"Sorry, Micah," J shouted back. "You should have paid attention to us earlier! Now you're on your own."

Within twenty seconds, the entire town square had cleared. No adoring crowds. No reporters. No cameramen.

Just Micah. Stuck on top of a horse.

He figured he should probably get off, but then he wasn't sure what he was supposed to do with the horse. He couldn't just leave it there. And besides, he wasn't sure he could get down even if he wanted to.

Maybe he'd ride it home, and then return it once the rain stopped. Yes, that seemed like a smart idea. But just like the last time he sat in this seat, he had no idea how to get the thing started.

It was probably voice-activated.

"Take me to 102 Oaklawn Court."

Nothing.

"Please?" he added, remembering his manners.

The horse's ears twitched backward, but nothing else moved. Without getting off, Micah looked the animal over—up and down from head to tail. Surely there were instructions somewhere. Or maybe a power button?

"A little help here?" he shouted, at no one in particular. "Anyone? . . . Tech support?"

FAME

The crowds love me.
Reporters want to interview me!
Photographers want photos of me!
And Chet can't touch me.
I'm on top of the world!

You might be asking, "But Micah, what about the crowds of people believing the lies . . . YOUR lies?!" What they don't know can't hurt them . . . right?

But what would happen if they found out I made it all up? They'd be so angry. I'd be in DEEP TROUBLE. On second thought, maybe this mess of lies isn't worth a few minutes of fame . . .

You may be sure that your sin will find you out.
Numbers 32:23 (NLT)

▷ **Why do YOU think Micah is confused about how he should feel?**

▷ **What would YOU do if you were getting attention for the wrong reasons?**

CHAPTER EIGHT

"Thanks for giving me a ride, Dad."

"No problem, Micah. But I still don't understand why you had me come get you at Olden Days Carriage Rides, and why Mr. Beckett thanked you for returning his horse."

"It's a long story. Can I tell you tomorrow? I'm exhausted."

"That would be fine, Micah." He looked over at his son sympathetically. "I'm beginning to suspect being a tour guide is more complicated than I thought."

"You have no idea."

Micah stared out the window, watching cars pass. A black sedan was heading the other direction, driven by a man in a suit and dark glasses. The sun had set over an hour ago.

Nah, it couldn't be one of Armin's government men. This was just some weirdo who liked wearing sunglasses at night. Right? Should he tell his dad about these men in suits? No, he couldn't. Because then he'd have to tell him all about his lies—how one lie about getting a good grade turned into more and more lies just to cover it up. If he didn't come completely clean, it wouldn't make sense that these men were coming after him. If they were. He still wasn't sure. Maybe the appearance of these mysterious men had nothing to do with him at all. But that sure seemed unlikely.

Micah was starting to get scared and really wanted his dad's help. But it felt like there was a wall between them because he couldn't tell him the truth.

His dad was right: being a tour guide really was more complicated than you'd think. Especially when you stretched the truth. Or, more accurately, straight-up lied.

But often problems don't seem nearly as scary in the daylight.

That Sunday afternoon, Micah, Lydia, Armin, and Gabe biked down to SmoothieTown, which was just off the town square. After ordering orange slime smoothies, they found an empty table by the window. Life was good. The skies were clear and the streets were crowded—a perfect day for people watching.

And an even better day if you happened to want people to be watching you.

Every few minutes another stranger would come up to their table and say hello to Micah or ask him if he'd mind giving them his autograph. He'd smile and say something humble, like "Not at all," or "Anything for my fans."

And every time he did, Lydia would roll her eyes and groan.

Finally, Micah was fed up. "Listen, Lydia. I can't help it if I happen to be a very entertaining tour guide!"

"It's pretty easy to entertain people if you don't care about the truth."

"You're just jealous of the awesome story about me in the paper!"

"Nobody reads the paper anymore."

Micah couldn't argue with that. "Well, I'm done with that stage of my life anyway. Mom says Mr. Leafblatt's ankle is all better now, and I've hung up my wig and hose."

"Not a day too early," Armin said. His eyes were darting around the room, looking like a rabbit caught in a dog pound.

Micah knew just what he was looking for.

"I've been seeing them a lot too."

"The men in suits and dark glasses?" Armin asked.

"Cian Safbi?" Gabe's eyes got big. "They're everywhere!"

Lydia looked at Armin. "What's he talking about?"

"I don't know what Gabe's talking about, but Micah and I are talking about government men," Armin answered. "We think they're after Micah! They're most likely CIA—I'm pretty sure they're the agents who'd be called in for this sort of thing."

"What sort of thing?"

"Oh, I don't know," said Armin sarcastically. "Maybe making up enormous lies about the history of Middletown—no, the entire nation!"

"Sheesh! Calm down, Armin," Micah said.

"Calm down? You're putting us all in danger!

They might think I'm an accomplice! And there goes my career in politics."

"You want to be a politician?" Lydia asked.

"I like to keep my options open."

Lydia shook her head. "You're all being ridiculous. First of all, there's no way the CIA, or any other government agency, cares about Micah's stupid lies. And second, even if they did, there's no way they'd send a bunch of mysterious men all the way down here to little old Middletown to secretly follow you for days. They'd just call the local police and have them tell you to stop. And if you really are breaking some kind of tourist code, they'd go ahead and arrest you."

"You think I am? Breaking the law, that is?"

"No, I don't think what you're doing is illegal. Just idiotic."

"Good." Micah breathed a sigh of relief. "I can live with being idiotic."

Armin nodded. "You have for years."

"I'm not sure I understand what's going on," said Gabe. "Who does Cian Safbi work for again?"

Lydia, Armin, and Micah all stared at him.

"Probably the Effluvians," Micah answered finally.

Gabe nodded. "Makes sense. They're behind everything these days!"

Lydia shook her head. "Micah! Seriously! You just can't seem to stop making things up, can you?"

But no one was listening anymore. A man had walked through the SmoothieTown door, stealing their attention. And it was one of *them*. Black suit. Dark glasses.

He walked briskly up to the counter and ordered a coffee. Black. It figured. Then he headed for a back corner and slid into a booth. Because of the sunglasses covering his eyes, Micah and his friends couldn't see if he was looking their direction or not.

"I still don't believe your theory," Lydia said. "But there's definitely something weird going on. What kind of a man can resist ordering a smoothie from SmoothieTown?"

Other Bad Things the Effluvian Empire May or May Not Be Responsible For

- Socks getting lost in the dryer
- The chemical attraction between spaghetti sauce and white shirts
- The annoying fact that foods that taste good are usually bad for you and foods that taste bad are usually good for you
- The way every time you switch lanes at the grocery store, you somehow end up in the slow lane
- Elvis's "death" and later reappearance in mattress commercials
- The invention of the spork, which somehow fails to do its job both as a spoon and as a fork
- Middletown's rotten cantaloupe smell
- The Cleveland Browns

"The Effluvians must've brainwashed him!" yelled Gabe. "We can't let them win!"

Micah ignored him. "So, what's your theory, Lydia?"

"First of all, I don't think these guys have anything to do with you, Micah"—she glanced at Armin—"And Armin, I think you're paranoid."

"I like being paranoid," said Armin. "It's kept me alive for ten years now."

Lydia rolled her eyes, then looked back at Micah. "I'm sure these guys are in town for something else. It has nothing to do with your ridiculous lies. They're probably just here for some boring reason, like somebody in the upper levels of Middletown government being in trouble for tax evasion or embezzlement."

"I don't know what those words mean," said Micah. "But they definitely sound boring. Here's hoping you're right!"

Armin's eyes still hadn't left the man in the suit. "I don't care what you say, Lydia. Everyone in here is either a kid or a mom. If your theory was right, there would be no reason for the suit to be staking this place out. Unless, of course, you think the government now cares about fifth graders not paying taxes from their lemonade stands."

"Either way," said Micah, "I'm going to the bathroom. Then we can head out and hopefully not be followed."

Micah was drying his hands when he thought he heard someone outside the bathroom door. Without even stopping to think, he immediately rushed into one of the stalls and locked the door behind him. What was he doing? He must've come down with a case of Armin's paranoia.

He heard the bathroom door open and peeked through the crack between the stall and the door. Sure enough, the man in the black suit had walked in. Maybe he wasn't so paranoid after all! Micah watched him go to the sink and wash his hands. But he was washing them strangely, never looking down at the water, instead staring into the mirror. The dark glasses made it impossible to see what he was looking at, but Micah knew. He was staring at the stalls to figure out where Micah was.

Slowly, without making a sound, Micah stepped up onto the toilet seat so his feet wouldn't show if the suited man looked under the stalls. Suddenly, the bathroom door opened again. Micah couldn't see the door anymore, since he was standing on the toilet, but he heard a familiar voice clear his throat—Armin!

What a good friend! He was risking his own neck and future political career to look out for Micah.

But what now? Micah wondered. Who would make the next move?

The man in the suit did. To Micah's surprise, he entered one of the stalls.

But why? If he was looking for Micah, why would he actually go into a stall? On the other hand, if he and Armin were being paranoid and this guy was just there to use the bathroom, then why would he wash his hands *before* he actually . . . you know . . . used the bathroom?

But maybe he was going in the stall to do something else, like load a gun! After all, he wouldn't

want to do that out in the open, with Armin as a witness.

Better yet, maybe he went into one of the stalls so he could secretly peek underneath the stall's wall, peering down the whole row of stalls to see if there were any feet showing. That way Armin wouldn't see him acting so suspiciously. Yes, that made sense! In fact, Micah could hear the man now, moving around in a way that didn't seem like normal bathroom stall procedures.

Micah had to make a move fast! He needed the element of surprise or he'd never make it out alive! With a burst of energy, he jumped off the toilet toward the stall door—and banged *right into* the door and crumpled to the floor in front of the toilet.

Guess it would have helped if he'd remembered to unlock the door first.

But there was no time to feel sorry for himself! With a second burst, Micah scrambled up, unlocked the stall, slammed the door open wide, and sprinted to the bathroom door.

The suited man was ready for him. He must've heard Micah's first try at bursting through the stall door and figured out he was trying to make a break for it. Luckily, Armin had figured this out too. Armin hurried down the row of stalls, "accidentally" blocking the exit of the man in the suit who "just happened" to be coming out of his stall at the same time.

As Micah rushed out of the bathroom, he could hear Armin's apologetic voice behind him as he blocked the man's path: "Excuse me. So sorry. I keep getting in your way. I did it again! How about we both go left? Silly me, I meant your left, not my left. You just stand there and I'll go around . . ."

Outside the bathroom, Micah realized he couldn't go through SmoothieTown's front door. Surely that was being watched. So, Micah ran to the back.

He nodded at the shocked smoothie artists as he swung through the saloon doors to the kitchen, rushing out the back door to an alley. On the other side of the alley were the back entrances to several other stores: the Yarn Barn, Soap Dispenser Emporium, and Everything Plaid. The question was, which way should he go? First, he looked to his right. Nothing there. But turning to his left, he saw a shadow. Probably just a raccoon. A very tall raccoon . . . wearing a suit? Probably not.

Micah took off to the right as fast as he could!

Out he burst from the shadowy alley into a broad avenue bathed in bright sunlight. He looked around, hoping for a crowd to blend into. A block ahead of him, people were gathered around a guy in a corn dog suit, giving out free samples. Micah ran up to them, hoping to get lost in their midst. But just before he got there, he heard the sirens.

He looked up to see black vans with mounted lights coming from his right and left. All he could do was run straight ahead down a side street.

Just then, another black van came straight toward him. And worse, he heard something even more frightening above him—chopper blades. With the van headlights blinding him, Micah fell to his knees, hands high in the air.

He was surrounded. It was the end of the line.

How Did I Get Here?

What would the FBI want from me? I know I lied . . . a lot. But shouldn't they have more important criminals to catch?

I never thought a simple red line would lead me here, surrounded by government goons, awaiting a fate that is sure to be worse than an F on a history test.

Nothing in all the world can be hidden from God. Everything is clear and lies open before him. Hebrews 4:13 (ICB)

▷ **Have YOU ever been caught in a lie? How did it feel?**

▷ **Why do YOU think it's impossible to hide something from God?**

CHAPTER NINE

Micah was not enjoying the van ride. He was terrified out of his mind and had just downed a 22-ounce smoothie, so it was all he could do to keep from opening his mouth and spraying the inside of the van with orange slime. Maybe he should warn the driver his van seats were about to get slimed—he couldn't imagine that being an easy stain to get out of upholstery. But he also couldn't imagine them being willing to stop and find a restroom on the way to wherever they were going.

Where *were* they going, anyway? At first Micah tried to keep his bearings. But between feeling a little dizzy and having a lousy sense of direction even under the best of circumstances, he lost track of where they were after about three turns.

There were two agents in the back of the van with him. They were the two who'd grabbed him in the first place—one was taller than the other, but both were big enough to be terrifying. Then there was the agent in the driver's seat. All three wore the uniform he'd grown used to by this time—black suits, black sunglasses, black shoes, and expressions that were . . . not expressions at all. He'd seen more emotion on the mannequins at MegaMart.

But there was also one other man in the van who didn't look like an agent. He sat in the passenger seat and wasn't dressed like the others. Micah couldn't see his face—just the back of his head—but he was a big man in a pinstripe suit and fedora. Maybe he was in charge of this whole operation.

As Micah looked from one person to another, all he could think about was what kind of trouble he was in, and what kind of punishment they had in mind.

Likely Sentences For My Crimes

- Being driven around in the van on a bunch of curvy roads until I puke up my orange slime smoothie.

- Being buried in endless red tape. (I heard about this on a lawyer show on TV, and it sounded awful.)

- Never letting me play video games except ones with unicorns and princesses.

- Two words: pantyhose wedgie.

- Life sentence in Alcatraz. Or was it Azkaban? I can never remember which one is real.

Micah's fears were growing and growing. He didn't know if he could hold back a scream any longer. Or his smoothie, for that matter. Something had to give!

Finally, he shouted at the top of his lungs: "What is happening? Where are you taking me?"

Micah's words seemed to echo in the tight space of the van. No one responded for a second or two. But then, as if in slow motion, the man in the passenger seat turned his head.

Micah couldn't believe it! It was Mayor Kim!

"We have a few questions for you, Mr. Murphy."

These were the first words anyone had spoken to him since his capture. The agents had grabbed him, led him by the arms to the van, and whisked him away in silence. No "You're under arrest." No "We work for the CIA." No "Please come with us." It was rude, come to think of it.

The mayor went on. "We're concerned about what we're hearing from you and want to know who you are and what's going on."

He spoke calmly, which to Micah made his words all the more frightening.

Micah stayed silent. He'd watched enough movies to know that's what heroes always do in these situations, to protect whatever information they're hiding. But that wasn't really why he clammed up. After all, he didn't even know if he *had* any information—he generally didn't. And even if he did, he would have given it up in a heartbeat to get out of whatever mess he was in.

No, he stayed silent because he didn't understand the question. Obviously, the mayor knew his name— they'd just called him Mr. Murphy. So how was he supposed to answer his question about who he was? And as for what was going on, he didn't have a clue. It felt like every class he'd ever been in, with grown-ups asking questions and him feeling dumb for not knowing the answers.

"So, you think you can hold out on us?" asked the taller agent. "Oh, we'll get you to talk. I have no doubt about that."

The shorter agent grinned an evil grin. "And you won't like our methods, Mr. Murphy."

Now Micah had even less of a clue what to say. What did they want from him? But he didn't have time to think it through and come up with a plan. Instead, they just started peppering him with questions.

"Who told you about Mayor McGillicutty?" the shorter agent asked.

"How did you know about the redacted manila memorandum?" asked the taller one.

"What else do you know about the Effluvian Empire?"

"Or maybe you have ties to the Effluvian Empire yourself!"

What? So they thought he actually knew some sort of secrets about the government and what was going on in the world? Was that why they were after him?

Suddenly the mayor joined in. "I don't know who's leaking information to you, Mr. Murphy, but it stops right now. And if you besmirch the good name of Middletown any longer, I will ruin you! Do you understand me?"

For the most part, Micah understood. He had no idea what "besmirch" meant, but the part about ruining him was pretty clear.

Micah suddenly realized he was in worse trouble than he'd even imagined. His head was spinning. His stomach was churning harder and harder, and he wanted someone to give him a clue about what was going on. Without thinking, he shouted out, "Where's my good cop?"

There was a moment of confused silence. The taller agent broke it first. "What are you talking about?"

Micah sighed. "You know. 'Good cop, bad cop.' I want my good cop. In all the TV shows, there's always a good cop and a bad cop, and neither one of you is my good cop. I want to know where my good cop is. I have a constitutional right to one . . . I think."

A stern look came over the shorter agent's face.

"Oh, so that's how you're going to play it? Well, there are no good cops around here. Just angry ones."

"We're not playing around, Mr. Murphy," the mayor shouted. "This is a matter of national security!"

The shorter agent banged a hand on the van door in frustration. "So, tell us what you know!"

"Right now!" the taller agent added.

"There's no way a judge will go easy on you if you refuse to talk!"

"We've already got everything we need to put you away for good, so you might as well confess. But time's running out. I've about had it with your tough-guy routine."

"I was afraid it would come to this," said the mayor. "Let's move to stage two of the interrogation."

Stage two? Sweat was pouring down Micah's face. He knew these guys were serious, but he didn't know what he was supposed to tell them. Micah didn't think things could get any worse!

But somehow, they managed to.

Suddenly the van stopped. Micah looked out the window.

Unfortunately, he now knew *exactly* where they were.

One of the agents in the back of the van grabbed Micah's arm, pulled him out of the vehicle, and led him up the sidewalk to his front door. He would have thought coming home to his parents would make him feel better—safer and more secure. But after all the lying, home no longer felt safe. And now he was not only in trouble with the United States government—even worse, his parents would be disappointed in him!

The shorter agent rang the bell. Micah heard footsteps coming to the door.

His mother opened it. "Oh! What is happening?"

Micah could see Audrey and his dad on the couch in the living room. Audrey was reading book 3 of the Amish Vampire Chronicles. His dad was reading the paper and now looked up for the first time. "Oh! Micah? What's going on? Mayor Kim?"

"Mr. and Mrs. Murphy, we've been questioning your son," said the mayor.

Micah's dad shook his head sadly. "Micah, I told you not to light firecrackers on public property!"

"That's not what we're here about," said the taller agent. "Perhaps you should have a seat."

"Can I get you anything to drink?" Micah's mom offered on their way to the dining room. "Or a snack? I've made mini muffins."

Micah sighed. There was nothing more

humiliating than his mom welcoming his accusers with open arms. And mini muffins.

Thankfully, the agents politely declined.

Micah sat at the table with his mom, dad, and the mayor. The agents all remained standing. Audrey stayed in the other room, somehow still reading her book. Micah couldn't help but be a little impressed with her ability to block things out. If only he'd had that skill when he should have been studying for the stupid history test!

Micah's thoughts were interrupted as the mayor started explaining things to his parents. "In his role as tour guide, your son has been sharing . . . er . . . sensitive information about Middletown and its leadership."

"Is this about your tamale incident?" Micah's dad asked. "I thought everyone already knew about that."

"It's not about the tamale!" the mayor snapped. Then he took a breath and composed himself.

The taller agent broke in. "He's been reporting things about a certain redacted envelope. And your local government's ties to the Effluvian Empire—"

"*Former* ties, that is," the mayor interrupted.

"Yes, of course," the taller agent said. "And we just don't know where it's all coming from."

"And more important," said the mayor, starting to lose his cool once again, "we want the leaks stopped!"

"Micah?" his dad asked. "What's all this about? What do you know, and where did your information come from?"

"Just tell the truth, Micah," his mom said. "We've always taught you to tell the truth."

Suddenly Micah's stomach was churning harder than ever. Why did she have to say that?

"We're starting to lose patience," said the taller agent.

The shorter one nodded. "The next step is questioning you at headquarters."

"You better tell us quick," the mayor said through gritted teeth. "Things will only get tougher on you if you play dumb."

Dumb? It kept coming back to that, didn't it? Micah couldn't take another second. In a burst of words, every bit of the truth poured out of him.

"I'm not *playing* dumb—I really *am* dumb! That's just it! I got a zero on my history test, so I used a red pen to turn it into a 100%, and just like that, everyone thought I was smart, so kids asked me to tutor them, and my dad wanted me to be president and Mr. Turtell had me join the Quiz Bowl—where I knew absolutely nothing—but luckily I puked just

in time, and I thought it was almost over, but then my mom pressured me into becoming a Middletown tour guide, but I didn't really know anything about local history, so I started making things up about the buildings and the bridges and the water towers and the mayor—whatever I could think of I'd say to the tourists—and for some reason, instead of laughing at me or kicking me out of town, they ate it up and I got huge crowds and the news did stories on me, and then these guys in dark suits and sunglasses started following me, and . . . oh, wait . . . you know about that last part already.

"So, the thing is," Micah went on, "I lied about everything. Ever since I got my history test back, almost every word out of my mouth has been untrue. One lie turned into another, bigger lie, until I just couldn't stop. I don't have any secret knowledge. I'm just a liar."

Micah took a deep breath. He didn't know if the truth would be enough to fix this problem, but boy oh boy, did it feel good to get it all off his chest.

The agents turned away from Micah. One of them seemed to be muttering to someone Micah couldn't see. Then Micah could hear very soft voices come through their earpieces, too soft to hear what they were saying. The agents nodded several times in silence. Finally, they looked back at Micah.

"His story checks out."

The mayor still didn't look happy. "Well, Mr. Murphy . . ."

"Yes?" said Micah's dad.

"Sorry . . . I meant the younger Mr. Murphy."

"Yes?" said Micah.

"We're going to need to fix this. Publicly. You will say to the press exactly what we tell you to say, nothing more, nothing less."

"Actually," said his mom, calmly but firmly, "how about he just tells the press the truth? About how he made stuff up because he was embarrassed. I'll not have him saying any more than the truth."

The mayor looked down at his shoes, almost like

he was a little embarrassed himself. "That will be fine, Mrs. Murphy."

Maybe the mayor *was* embarrassed, but no one could be more embarrassed than Micah was. His parents' disappointment—which was clear on their faces—was more painful than any consequence the agents would have delivered. He knew he was about to get what he had coming for all the lying and masquerading as a "boy genius." And if that weren't embarrassing enough, he knew the agents knew it too. They'd probably laugh all the way to the Pentagon—or wherever they were from.

You Can't Make This Stuff Up!

What were the odds that the stuff I made up about the town was actually true? Does that mean I WASNT lying?! At least the truth is out and I don't have to make up any more lies. Those government agents will finally leave me alone! But now . . . now I have to face my parents . . .

Out of the frying pan and into the fire . . .

No discipline is enjoyable while it is happening–it's painful! But afterward there will be a peaceful harvest of right living for those who are trained in this way.
Hebrews 12:11 (NLT)

 Why do YOU think Micah is relieved that the truth is finally out?

 What good things have YOU learned through discipline and consequences?

CHAPTER TEN

Once the agents and the mayor had left, Micah's parents let him have it.

"I can't believe you'd ever do something like this, Micah!" his dad said.

"What were you thinking?" His mom shook her head in disappointment.

"What do you have to say for yourself, young man?" His dad again.

"Ummm . . . umm . . . ," Micah stammered.

"We expect more out of you than"—his dad was at a loss for words—"than . . . *this*!" He looked over his shoulder at Micah's sister.

Audrey hadn't moved from the couch. "Honestly, I can't believe Micah could do something like this," she said, not looking up from her book. "It's shocking," she added, in her usual sarcastic tone.

"And what about all those poor tourists, hanging on your every word?" his mother said. "They've been duped! They will feel like fools when they find out about your lies. You're going to give every one of them their tips back!"

"But . . . how?" Micah asked. "I don't know any of them or where they live."

"Well . . . then you're going to give all your tip money back to the town!"

Micah didn't know how to respond. Even his sister glanced up from her book to look at them strangely.

His dad didn't miss a beat. "I can't believe this, Micah! We were so proud of you for finally working hard and getting an A."

"The sky was the limit!" said his mom.

"There goes becoming a college professor!"

"There goes the presidency!"

"We're just so disappointed!" sighed his dad.

"You've let your family down," said his mother.

"Yeah," added Audrey, yawning as she turned the page in her book. "I've never felt so ashamed."

"Please," said his mother, "just explain why you did it."

Micah hated his parents' look of disappointment. "I just couldn't believe how bad I did on the history test. It was the worst grade in the whole class, and I felt humiliated. I started to panic, and I couldn't figure out a solution other than to lie. And then one lie turned into another lie, and another. It was out of my control! There wasn't a way out."

To Micah's surprise, his dad gave him a look of sympathy. "Micah," he said, "I want you to listen to me carefully right now. There is *always* a way out. Lying is never the answer."

His mom nodded. "How do you think God feels about lying, Micah?"

"It makes Him mad," Micah said sheepishly.

"And sad," his mom added. "Because in the end, lying doesn't just hurt the people that are lied to—it also hurts the liar."

"You can say that again!" said Micah. "I've never been so scared in my whole life!"

His dad sighed. "Well, Micah, I'm glad you've learned a lesson, but there are still consequences for what you've done. You're definitely not going to Pukey Pete's."

Micah hung his head. "I understand."

That night, for the first time in a long time, Micah could be totally honest again on his vlog. He confessed to his followers what he'd done and apologized for embarrassing them—or, more accurately, embarrassing himself in front of them. He also explained how God feels about lying. Lying never works out in the end, and God knows it. He wants the best for us, Micah said, but lies will only lead to trouble.

It was the hardest post he'd ever created. But it

was also one of the best. A great weight had been lifted that he didn't even know he'd been carrying around. And when it was all said and done, he didn't even care about how many "likes" he received. He was just relieved the truth was finally out there!

The next morning before school, the mayor organized a press conference, as he'd promised. Micah recognized most of the same cameramen, reporters, and news anchors he'd seen when he was a popular tour guide—including Stormy McAllister and PB and J—but now they all looked angry at being lied to rather than excited to be in the presence of a cool new celebrity. They probably felt pretty dumb. Micah could relate to that.

His stomach was churning as he stepped in front of the crowd. But there was no backing down now.

"I'm so sorry for all the lies I told as a tour guide," Micah told them. "I wasn't getting any secret inside information. Everything I said about the town's history, I just made up. I want to apologize to the tourists, the media, and to the mayor."

The media, to his surprise, didn't have any follow-up questions. Apparently, they just wanted to put it all behind them—probably because they were embarrassed too.

"Kids these days," grumbled one of the reporters as he walked away.

Another one chimed in: "At least we won't have any more idiots walking around town in a wig and hose."

Armin and Lydia had been watching the press conference from the back. They came up to Micah as the crowds left. He hadn't had a chance to talk to them since SmoothieTown.

"So, what happened with the agents?" Armin asked.

"They questioned me about how I found out about the redacted manila envelope and former Mayor McGillicutty's ties to the Effluvian Empire."

"How you 'found out about' that stuff?" Lydia asked making air quotes with her fingers. "Are you saying . . . it was real?"

"Maybe," said Micah. "I don't really understand it all, but apparently I was close enough to the truth to make them uncomfortable. The world's a crazy place, I guess."

"Well," said Lydia. "I'm proud of you for telling the truth. I felt like we were losing the real you with all the lies piling up."

"Yeah," said Armin. "Even if you fail at something like a test, being honest about it helps you grow and learn. And you know we'll always be your friends, no matter how badly you do on your grades."

"Deep down I knew that about you guys, but it's good to hear you say it out loud."

Lydia smiled at Micah. "And I can't believe how bravely you told the truth in front of all those cameras and reporters! You were incredible."

"I know how to handle the press," Micah said confidently.

But he immediately regretted it.

Without warning, his churning stomach caught

up to him. Up came his breakfast and maybe even his dinner from the night before.

Micah smiled. True relief at last! "I've been trying to hold that down since yesterday."

As soon as Micah walked into class the next morning, Mr. Turtell asked him to come up to his desk. Micah figured he'd probably heard all about what happened, but there was always a chance he hadn't. Mr. Turtell, after all, was usually last in line when it came to the spread of interesting school gossip.

No such luck. Just by the look on his face, Micah could tell the truth had somehow made its way to him.

"Your last test grade has gone back to being a zero, of course," Mr. Turtell said. "That means you better do well on Thursday's test. It's worth another third of your grade."

"Yes, Mr. Turtell. What do I need to get on it?"

"You'll need at least a C+ to avoid a failing grade on your report card."

"Okay," Micah said. He started to walk back to his desk, but turned himself back around. "And I'm really sorry for what I did. I don't know what got into me."

"Well, now you've learned a valuable lesson about history—something that's true of kings and queens, great generals, artists, philosophers, and even just regular folks like us."

"What's that, Mr. Turtell?"

"In the short term, you might be able to fool people. But eventually, no matter how smart you are, the truth about who you really are always seems to come out." Mr. Turtell shrugged.

Huh, Micah thought to himself. Wise words.

Mr. Turtell might not be as absent-minded as he'd believed. Micah didn't know what else to say, so he just walked back to his seat, avoiding the stares of his classmates as much as he could. He knew there was absolutely no chance that *they* hadn't heard the news.

The speed of light is the fastest thing in the universe. The speed at which embarrassing news about a fifth grader travels through New Leaf elementary is a close second.

On his way back to his desk, Micah was glared at by some and intentionally ignored by others. He'd been glared at and ignored by his classmates before, but he'd never deserved it so much. And that somehow made it feel worse.

Micah sat down and noticed several kids giggling around him. He felt his back for a Kick Me sign, but there was nothing there. He looked all over his desk and book bag to see if there was anything else embarrassing. Nothing. At last he stood up and looked at his chair. In

7 Degrees of Being Shunned in Fifth Grade

1. Your classmates give you the silent treatment.

2. They pick you last in gym.

3. They leave your picture out of the yearbook...

4. ...unless you get a bad haircut. Then they put your picture on every page of the yearbook.

5. The person in front of you in the lunch line takes the last of the tater tots.

6. You're not invited to classmates' birthday parties.

7. You're not even invited to your own birthday party.

red lipstick—no doubt swiped from his mom—Hanz had written "liar" backwards. Why backwards? It only took Micah a few seconds before he figured it out. He stretched around so he could see the back of his shorts. Sure enough, the word "liar" was written across his backside, for all the world to see.

PB looked at Micah. "You figured that out pretty quick for a guy about to fail fifth grade."

Beside him, J shook her head. "I can't believe we interviewed you for our show! What a waste."

"A waste of what?" Lydia asked.

"Of . . . celebrity!"

Micah couldn't disagree. At the moment he would've preferred not to be famous anyway. He felt eyes on the back of his head and turned around. Chet was staring a hole through him.

"You don't have your fans to protect you anymore!" he growled under his breath.

"But at least now you know I'm not really a nerd," Micah said. "That's a mark in my favor, right?"

"It's true that I hate nerds," said Chet. "But at

least I respect them. Unlike liars. You're not even worth a wedgie!"

"Man, I never thought I'd miss a wedgie," Micah sighed.

"Well, I still respect you, Micah!" Gabe said.

"Thanks, Gabe!" Micah responded. "I really appreciate it."

"Someone's gotta be on your side against the Effluvians!"

"But—," Micah started to say.

Armin cut him off. "I wouldn't bother. He's in his own world, and it seems like a happy place."

"I'd join him if I could," Micah said.

This Isn't Me

Well, my parents are disappointed in me, my classmates think I'm a liar, and even though I apologized at the press conference, I'm sure the rest of Middletown aren't fans either.

But who can blame them? I lied. Over and over again. That is probably the most honest thing I've said in a while! But I don't want to BE a liar... And thankfully, because of God, I don't have to. When I tell Him what I've done, He forgives me ... He changes me. And with His help, I can make better decisions in the future.

If we confess our sins, he is faithful and just to forgive us our sins and to cleanse us from all unrighteousness.
1 John 1:9 (ESV)

▷ **How have YOU felt after admitting your mistakes to God?**

▷ **Why do YOU think it's important that Micah understands—this is not who he is?**

CHAPTER ELEVEN

Thursday's test was about state history, a subject Micah knew nothing about. But he paid attention in class on Tuesday and Wednesday, which made two days in a row—a new record! He'd never paid attention for more than . . . well, he'd never paid attention. Even Mr. Turtell's turtles couldn't distract him! Micah had to keep reminding himself that anything he doesn't learn in class was something he'd have to learn at home—on his own time. He'd learned that the hard way on his last test. He wasn't going to let that happen again.

Unfortunately, Lydia and Armin were so busy

they couldn't study with him, so he was on his own. But maybe that was good—studying by himself was a skill he needed to master. Every night that week, after doing his chores and eating his dinner, he spent time in his room, actually reading his textbook and looking over his notes. Sure, there were the usual distractions—messy floors, missing toys, out-of-town squirrels—but he somehow managed to push all that aside and focus.

Well, he managed to focus in short bursts, at least. At one point he read for a good fifteen minutes straight without stopping. He was breaking records left and right!

And it was horrible. Studying, he discovered, was a lot of work. In fact, he hadn't remembered working so hard in his life—except maybe that time he had to learn how to use his camera to record the talent show. He was used to what it felt like when his muscles were tired, like when he had to run the mile in gym. And he'd known what it felt like for his thumbs to be tired from playing video games

Distractions I Somehow Managed to Ignore (for which I deserve a medal)

- A puffy white cloud shaped exactly like Captain Karate Dino Cop
- Audrey sneaking out of her bedroom by a rope dangling in front of my window
- A fight between a possum and a raccoon in my tree house
- A phone call from Q104 letting me know I'd won two tickets to Monster Truck-stravaganza
- An ice cream truck broken down in front of my driveway while children screamed, "Free ice cream! Best day ever!"

for hours. But he'd never known what it was like for his brain to feel tired. How did other kids stand this torture, night after night? Maybe they did stuff to exercise their brains somehow so they didn't get worn-out so easily.

No, that was ridiculous.

But he made it through the hard work, he fought through the distractions, and he got the job done. And when Thursday morning came, he was ready!

The test was all essay questions, and this time none of them caught him completely by surprise. He wasn't sure he knew all the answers, but at least he wasn't making any of them up off the top of his head—everything he wrote about came from his notes or from the textbook. Whether or not his answers matched the questions was up for debate, but at least there was no mention of smoothies or weasels.

On Friday morning, Micah woke up with a stomachache. He knew Mr. Turtell would be passing out their tests, and he had no idea what to expect.

Did he get every question right? Not even close! Did he get most of them right? Well . . . maybe. He felt like he could be anywhere between a D+ and an A–. That was a broad range of grades, he realized, but with essay questions it was so hard to feel confident.

He rushed through breakfast, barely eating a bite, and actually made it to school early for a change. Which meant he had to wait.

He hated waiting.

The rest of the class rolled in one by one, talking quietly among themselves or finishing up homework from the night before. Gabe waved when he arrived, but other than that everyone ignored Micah. He was almost glad he was being shunned; he didn't really feel like chatting.

Just before the bell rang, Armin and Lydia slipped through the door and sat down. "How you feeling, Micah?" Armin asked.

"Nervous."

Lydia nodded. "That seems appropriate."

Mr. Turtell took an incredibly long time to

take attendance and an even longer time to make announcements that no one listened to. But after what felt like weeks of waiting, at last he returned the tests—upside down, as usual.

"I can't look," Micah squeaked to Armin and Lydia.

Armin snatched it off his desk and turned it over without Micah being able to see it. He looked at it without expression. "Remind me what you needed to not fail history?"

"A C+," Micah said.

"Oh."

Micah's heart sank in his chest.

Suddenly, Armin flipped it over. "You passed!" he said. "B–!"

"Wow! Really? That's great!"

"It *is* great, Micah," said Lydia, looking at the test over Armin's shoulder. She smiled. "And almost all your answers actually make sense!"

"You are smart!" said Armin.

Micah shrugged. "Well . . . smart enough."

Lydia nodded. "And the important thing is, you learned how to actually study, and it paid off. This is a big moment for you."

Gabe leaned over to look at Micah's grade. "Wow! Do you think your mom will frame it?"

"Probably not. But at least she'll know I earned it this time."

Word about Micah's test passed through the classroom. Most of his classmates didn't care—they were still angry with him for having made them believe he was some kind of genius. But others actually told him "good job." Things seemed to slowly be getting back to normal.

Chet leaned over to have a look at Micah's test for himself. "Well, now I'm torn. Are you a nerd or not? It's hard to tell. I guess I'll just have to give you a huge wedgie at recess anyway."

Micah sighed. "It seems like whatever happens, it always ends up with you giving me a huge wedgie."

Chet shrugged. "Life's funny that way."

At the end of the day, Micah walked out of the school's big front doors, looking for Armin and Lydia so they could walk home together. He had just gotten past the columns and was heading down the concrete steps when he heard a noise coming from the bushes on his left.

"Pssst. Over here."

It was Hanz. Rats. Hanz was the richest, snobbiest kid in school.

Hanz moved to Middletown from Germany a

few years before because his dad was some hotshot at a local technology company. Hanz got everything he ever wanted and liked to make people jealous. Nothing good ever came from a conversation with Hanz. Micah walked over to him anyway. Nothing good ever came from trying to ignore Hanz either.

"I've been vatching vat you've been doing vith ze press. Looks like you've really got zem fooled. So, is it all over vith? Did you clear your name vith ze FBI?" Hanz asked.

"I guess so."

"Good. Just remember, nobody likes a snitch."

"What?"

"You heard me. Better keep your mouz shut. No more leaks. If zey cut funding to my fazzer's bubble wrap technology program, you're in big trouble."

"Huh?"

"I'm not fooled. I know vat you know."

"About what?"

"Ze bubble wrap force field. Don't act dumb vith me."

"Why does everyone keep accusing me of *acting* dumb?! Like I told the reporters, I just made it all up!"

"Good. Keep talking zat way. It's best to keep up ze act. You never know who's listening."

Micah didn't know what to say to this. "Okay."

"And one more zing: you better not say anyzing to anyone about ze quantum fabrications conglomerate!"

"I couldn't if I wanted to."

"Okay zen. Ve see eye to eye on zis." Hanz nodded to Micah as he walked away. "Good talk."

And he was right. It was probably the best talk he'd ever had with Hanz, even though he barely understood a word of it.

Halfway down the street, Armin and Lydia were waiting for him.

"What was that all about?" Armin asked.

"I have absolutely no idea."

The Big "B"

I got a B on my history test! So, studying actually does pay off! It looks like I won't flunk out of history after all. Now if I can just get through my job at Pukey Pete's to pay back the tip money I got for being a tour guide, I can finally put this all behind me.

I should have just studied like this the first time around. It would have saved us all a lot of trouble!

And whatever you do, in word or deed, do everything in the name of the Lord Jesus, giving thanks to God the Father through him.
Colossians 3:17 (ESV)

▷ **Why do YOU think it felt good for Micah to get a B?**

▷ **Who should get the credit when we make the right choices?**

CHAPTER TWELVE

Today was the day, and it was time to dress for the occasion. Micah hated the thought of what he was about to wear, but he had no choice. After all, he had to pay the Middletown Historical Society back for being such a bad tour guide (not to mention all the tourists who were demanding their tip money back), and the only way he could do that was to get a job. In Middletown, there was only one option: he had to be Barfie, the Pukey Pete mascot.

Barfie was a giant barf bag that walked around the amusement park, giving out purple cotton candy to little kids. It was probably the worst job in all of Middletown.

But he had to admit, he deserved it. His lying had consequences. His web of lies had grown and grown until it exploded all over the town, and now he had to clean up the mess he'd made. Who could have guessed it would all end up with him dressing like a giant barf bag? Life is full of surprises.

But if he had to do it, he might as well own it. Hold his head high. Wear the costume with pride. Become the best Barfie the world had ever seen. Maybe it wouldn't be so bad. After all, when his mom first made him dress up like a colonial Middletonian, he had thought it was going to be terrible, with the hose and the wig and whatnot. But that turned out great! Kind of . . . for a little while at least . . . and maybe this would turn out all right too.

Step-by-step, he took all the pieces of the Barfie costume out of the dry-cleaning bag and laid them out on his bed. Then he put on the outfit piece by piece, as if he were donning armor—oversized white gloves; huge, floppy shoes; and last but not least, a giant, brown foam suit that was shaped like a barf bag with big googly eyes. On the back of the bag was written Barfie's full name: "The Amazing Puke-tastic Barfolemew, aka, 'Barfie'!"

And just like that, the transformation was complete. He had put aside Micah and had become Barfie! It wasn't embarrassing—it was fun. An honor, even! Little children would look up to him, and older children would share a giggle when he passed. He was doing something important for the community!

But no matter how he tried to look at it, this was not Micah's proudest moment. He stared at himself in the mirror, adjusted his gloves, threw his shoulders back, and tried to strike the most confident pose he could manage.

Wow. There really was no possible way to look cool in this costume.

It would be embarrassing—humiliating, even—but he had to come to terms with that. This was part of the consequences of his lying, and if he was going to earn the town's trust back, he had to own up to what he'd done and face the music.

Micah walked out of his room with his head held high. Maybe he couldn't be proud of his costume, but he could be proud of the way he was handling his punishment.

Audrey looked up from her book as he strolled through the living room on his way out the door. "You forgot your pants."

Micah smiled. "Ha! You almost made me look."

"I'd recommend that you do."

He looked down. Rats. She was right.

A few minutes later, Micah headed out the door again, this time wearing everything he needed. Pukey Pete's was only four blocks from his house, so it only took him five minutes to get there, which was only five minutes later than he was supposed to arrive.

His manager, Bernice, was a drill sergeant of a woman who told him she'd worked there for thirty years and wouldn't take any guff from anyone. Micah didn't know what "guff" was, but he hadn't intended to give her any, so he figured they'd get along just fine. Bernice walked him through a brief orientation and training session, and then he was ready to walk around the park and start greeting guests.

There are a lot of humiliating things about dressing up like a giant barf bag: the oversized gloves sometimes get caught in doorways; the big, floppy shoes make you walk like a duck. But most of his responsibilities, it turned out, weren't all that horrible. He greeted guests at the entrance gate. He posed for pictures with children. He passed out candy and toy whistles. Everything you'd expect from an amusement park mascot. There was only one task that he absolutely hated: having to do the Barfie dance. Especially since he was not particularly coordinated.

The Barfie dance looks simple enough. Three hops to the left, three hops to the right, spin around

two times with your hands in the air, then hold your
stomach as you bow forward as far as you can. As
Barfie takes the bow, he pushes a button on the side
of the bag, and purple cotton candy shoots out the
top of the costume.

It's absolutely disgusting. The kids love it.

They all rush to Barfie like he's a busted piñata and grab as many baggies of cotton candy as they can, tearing open the packages and shoving the candy into their mouths before their parents can tell them to stop . . . or at least slow down.

It's all in good fun, of course. And in small doses, Micah probably could have handled it. But sometimes it was just too much.

Four hours into his day, Micah was asked to do the Barfie dance by a mob of second graders celebrating a birthday. With twenty-two kids in the party, not everyone had gotten cotton candy when he'd pushed the button, so they asked him to do the dance again.

Fine. Whatever. He did it again, and as he stood up from his final bow, Micah felt a little unsteady on his feet. But he was a true professional, so he walked away waving, never letting on that he'd almost fallen over right in front of them.

But he was no more than twenty feet away when

another troop of young kids—kindergartners and preschoolers this time—asked for the Barfie dance. As the children spun in front of him, Micah knew it wasn't a good idea for him to do it again, so he started to wave them off merrily and go on his way.

Then he caught his manager, Bernice's, eye. She had just happened to be walking by at the worst possible moment. He knew he couldn't refuse the children's request with her watching.

Three hops left.

Three hops right.

Spin around once.

Spin around a second time.

Stop spinning.

Wait . . . why couldn't he stop spinning? Or maybe he had. But then why was the world still going in circles?

Try to bow down low as he pushed the button.

Oh no! There was no way he was going to stay on his feet. The world was twisting around him, and he could barely figure out where he was going, but there were kids everywhere and nowhere to land. He tried to dodge, but the more he dodged, the dizzier he got. He could feel himself bouncing off preschoolers, knocking them down like bowling pins. Kids were shouting and laughing, thinking it was some crazy party game. Parents screamed, knowing he was about to knock over their precious babies.

Micah felt something cold and wet splash against his stomach and looked down to see a chunky, brown liquid dripping down his costume.

Some kid was yelling. "Hey! You made me spill my cookie dough milkshake!"

Micah bounced off him and tried to get away from the pack. But his costume was twisted now, and the eye holes weren't lined up anymore. He blindly pushed himself through the crowd until there was no one else around, and then banged his shins hard against a short concrete wall.

Something in him knew he needed to keep himself from falling forward. He had no idea where he was, but he had a sense he needed to step back.

But alas, his momentum was too much. In his dizzy state there was no way to turn himself around and back up. He started to tip forward, and it was all he could do to throw his hands in front of him so he didn't fall flat on his face.

Down he flipped over the wall, straight into the log flume pool.

The bad news was there wasn't a spare Barfie costume. Micah would have to walk around in a damp barf bag suit and wet, squeaky oversized shoes for the rest of his shift. But the good news was his accidental swim had broken the cotton candy button!

The rest of his shift was spent explaining to people that (A) they'd no longer get cotton candy when he did the Barfie dance, and (B) no, that wasn't real puke on his shirt—it was just a cookie dough milkshake.

At five o'clock, his shift ended. He'd seen Armin, Lydia, and Gabe several times at the park that day, but they hadn't been able to tell it was Micah in the Barfie costume. They had no idea he was even there.

But now it was time to let the world know he was Barfie. Micah caught up to his friends, who were drinking neon blue icees at the Snack Shack.

"Surprise!" he shouted.

"Um . . . ," Armin said, "surprise to you too, Barfie."

Apparently, they hadn't recognized his voice. Micah took the bag off his head and tried again. "Surprise!"

"Micah!" Lydia shouted. "I can't believe you'd sink to this level! I'm so proud of you!"

"Okay. That's a weird thing to say."

"No, I mean it's great that you're willing to embarrass yourself for a job. You've come a long way!"

"Yeah," Armin agreed. "It was the fact that you weren't willing to be embarrassed about a stupid test that got you into all this mess in the first place."

"I embarrass myself all the time!" Gabe said. "You get used to it."

Micah took off the rest of his costume so that he was just wearing the pants and T-shirt he'd worn underneath it all day. Unfortunately, he'd forgotten to bring a change of shoes, so he still had to wear the huge, Barfie ones.

Armin looked him up and down. "Why are you all wet?"

"It's a long story."

"Tough day at the office?" Lydia asked.

"You have no idea."

"I like your shoes!" Gabe said.

Suddenly Micah had an image of Gabe dressing like him, just like he had with the colonial outfit. "Just to be absolutely clear, Gabe, these shoes are part of the Barfie costume. It's not my new 'look'!"

Gabe shrugged. "If you say so."

Roller Coaster Hurl Index

Based on my experience (since I've been tall enough to ride) and years of watching and waiting for my turn to brave the rails, I've rated every Pukey Pete's CoasterTown coaster on a scale of one to five (see below for the fully detailed scale).

- Princess Twist-a-Lot BeDazzler: 1
- The Mind-Blender: 2
- Anti-Gravitron: 3
- The Flibbertigibbet: 3

- The Spin Cycle: 4
- Rage-a-holic Body-Slam Deluxe: 4
- The NOOOOOO!!!!!: 5

Scale for rating the roller coasters:

1 = Throw up in your mouth a little

2 = Lose your lunch

3 = Lose your lunch, your breakfast, and last night's dinner

4 = Lose your lunch, breakfast, last night's dinner, plus two meals you haven't even eaten yet

5 = May cause you to question ever eating again

"Okay," Lydia said. "Enough fashion talk. Let's get in line for the Spin Cycle again!"

"Let's ride the Ferris wheel instead!" exclaimed Gabe.

Armin rolled his eyes. "Only kids who bring their moms with them ride the lame Ferris wheel."

"Please?" Gabe begged. "I always puke on the Spin Cycle."

"Fine."

They got in the back of a very long line, but Micah didn't mind in the least. This was usually the worst part of amusement parks for him, but he was enjoying the freedom of being out of his costume so much that nothing else really mattered. He didn't have to look out of eye holes, and he could once again breathe fresh air without a costume covering his face. He even felt like the sun was shining just for him to dry off his wet clothes.

"Hey! Isn't that the kid who made up all that stuff about Middletown?"

"It sure looks like him."

Two older women walking down a lane nearby were staring at Micah. Soon others were staring and whispering too.

"Yeah," the first woman said, "I saw his picture in the paper! How humiliating!"

"No . . . that wasn't me . . . ," Micah started to say. But then he caught himself. It was amazing how lying could become like a reflex, something you did automatically whenever you're in a tough spot. He took a deep breath and changed his tune. "Yep. That was me. I'm embarrassed I did all that."

Everyone just looked at him, the expression on their faces saying they weren't sure what to say next.

"Well, you should be," the first woman said. She turned back to her friend and spoke more softly, but still loud enough for Micah to hear. "I can't believe what kids try to get away with these days."

"We would have never dared to do such a thing!" said her companion.

"Their parents let them get away with murder."

"Not to mention all those video games they play."

"And those weird clothes they wear."

"Just the other day, I saw kids walking down the street in colonial wigs!"

"And now they're wearing big, floppy shoes? What's that all about?"

Micah couldn't hear any more as the women walked away.

"That was weird," Armin said quietly.

"No, I deserved it," Micah answered. "I'm guessing I'll be getting that a lot for a while."

Gabe was in his own world, staring at Micah's feet. "I guess grown-ups just don't understand fashion these days."

The Ferris wheel was divided into six-person cars, so when Micah and his friends got up to the front of the line, they ended up sharing their car with a boy and his mom. The boy was a couple of years younger than Micah and looked a little embarrassed to be riding with his mother. He had a fake barbed wire tattoo on his arm, and wore ripped jeans and a concert T-shirt from the Downers Cold Cereal Tour.

The boy's mom, meanwhile, was wearing mom clothes.

"Aren't you Micah Murphy?" the boy asked.

Micah sighed. "Did you see me in the paper?"

"No, I know you from your vlog."

"Really?" Micah asked.

"*Really?*" Lydia repeated.

"Yeah, I love it!"

Micah looked at Lydia. "See, I told you I have

fans who aren't even friends or family!"

Lydia looked at the boy skeptically. "You're really, like, Micah's fan? Not his second cousin or something?"

"Not that I know of. But that would be so cool if I was!"

Micah smiled. "Well, it's good to meet a fan."

"Actually," the boy's mom added, "I wanted to thank you for sharing the post you made about coming clean and telling the truth."

"Uhh ... you're ... welcome?" Micah responded, sounding more like he was asking a question. He wasn't sure if she was being serious or not.

"That meant a lot to us, right, Brandon?"

The young boy, who was apparently named Brandon, shrugged and nodded. "Yeah. after I watched it, I confessed to my mom that I'd been taking change from her coin dish little by little. I'd saved up twenty dollars over the last year." He pointed at his fake arm tattoo. "I was about to turn this baby into a real one!"

"Well, I'm glad you came clean," Micah said.

"Me too," said Brandon. And he looked like he meant it. Micah wasn't surprised. He knew the relief that came with a clean conscience.

Micah glanced over at Armin and Lydia. Armin smiled and Lydia gave him a wink.

As the Ferris wheel slowly spun around, to his surprise, Micah found himself enjoying the ride. Sometimes it was good to just relax a little rather than always chasing a big thrill. And the wheel was huge—nearly as tall as a skyscraper—so at the top, Micah could see all the way across town. He saw his school, and maybe the roof of his house, if he was right about which street was his. He even thought he could see the street where he was first confronted by the agents. It had just happened the week before, but it already felt like years ago.

Micah looked down at the tiny, peaceful world below. Everything was so calm and quiet. All in all, it had been a good day. It was no picnic being Barfie, but better a giant barf bag than a liar. And now he was having fun with his friends. What else could he ask for? All was right with the world.

Except, of course, for Gabe sitting beside him, screaming in terror. But that was to be expected.

Micah and his friends were soon dropped onto the platform to get off the ride. They unbuckled themselves and walked away.

"That was all right," stated Micah.

"Whatever," said Lydia.

"Lame," added Armin.

"Are you kidding me? It was fantas—" Gabe started.

But the "tic" never came out of his mouth. Instead, neon blue icee did. All over his shirt, his shorts, and his shoes.

Micah and Armin just stared at him. Lydia shook her head. "Are you kidding me?"

Gabe ignored her. "Let's ride it again!"

The Ride of My Life

What a ride! I can't believe all that's happened this month:

1. A failed test

2. A quiz bowl

3. Wearing hose and a wig

4. A slow-moving horse

5. A ferris wheel

6. Being chased by the FBI!

It's like something out of a movie!

Have you ever gotten yourself caught up in a web of lies? Maybe your web wasn't as sticky as mine, but even the tiniest fibs can wreak havoc on our lives. I learned some really good lessons through this whole ordeal.

LYING IS NEVER A GOOD IDEA

No matter how small the lie may seem. I think I proved that little lies often lead to bigger ones. It's always best to be honest and own our shortcomings, differences, and the truth about who we are. Lying hurts God's heart, it hurts others (like our parents and friends), but mostly, we hurt ourselves and our reputation when we lie.

GOD FORGIVES OUR MISTAKES

We all mess up. We all make bad choices from time to time. But God loves us, and He's always there, ready to forgive us and help us do better next time.

I'm thankful my gig at Pukey Pete's was just temporary. I know I deserved that fate, but that costume! Having to spend a day in that costume was enough to make me rethink EVERYTHING I say from now on. I don't want to end up there again. I mean, I want to live in a way that pleases God—avoiding the Barfie costume is just an added bonus to living with integrity.

Finally, brothers, whatever is true, whatever is honorable, whatever is just, whatever is pure, whatever is lovely, whatever is commendable, if there is any excellence, if there is anything worthy of praise, think about these things. What you have learned and received and heard and seen in me—practice these things, and the God of peace will be with you.
Philippians 4:8-9 (ESV)

▷ **Which of the lessons Micah learned will be most helpful to YOU?**

▷ **What eight characteristics should guide our thoughts and actions according to Philippians 4?**

About the Author

Andy McGuire has written and illustrated four children's books, including *Remy the Rhino* and *Rainy Day Games*. He has a BA in creative writing from Miami University and an MA in literature from Ohio University. Andy's writing heroes have always been the ones who make him laugh, from Roald Dahl and Louis Sachar to P. G. Wodehouse and William Goldman. Andy lives with his wife and three children in Burnsville, Minnesota.

About the Illustrator

Girish Manuel is the creator of the Micah's Super Vlog video series and a producer at Square One World Media. He lives in a little place called Winnipeg, Canada, with his lovely wife, Nikki, and furry cat, Paska. Girish enjoys running and drawing . . . but not at the same time. That would be hard. He tried it once and got ink all over his shoes.

Have you ever felt bad for something you did?
We all do stuff that we shouldn't do.
Maybe we've told a lie, or even stolen something . . .
When we go our own way instead of God's, it's called **SIN**.
Sin keeps us from being close to God
and it has some other serious consequences . . .

but I've got some good news!

GOD LOVES YOU!

°Yes, the amazing,
incredible,
Creator who made the universe
and everything in it
(including YOU)
loves you!

How do I know this?

Because God is my friend. And He wants to be <u>your</u> friend too!

Check this out:

When we sin, the payment is death (Romans 6:23). But God gives us the gift of eternal life (John 3:16). That's because of what Jesus did for us on the cross.

What did Jesus do exactly?

Jesus, God's very own son, came down to earth to save us from our sin and restore our relationship with God! He did that by living a perfect life (without sin!) and taking the punishment for OUR sins when He was nailed to a cross (a punishment for really bad criminals back then)!

Jesus did this because He loved us enough to take OUR punishment! But that's not the end of the story. Three days after His death, Jesus rose from the grave, proving that God has power over sin and death!

So, what now?

Even though there's countless things we have done wrong, God can forgive our sins . . . no matter how many or how big they are! He wants to have a relationship with you through Jesus!

Check this out:

Everyone sins (Romans 3:23). No one measures up to God's glory. But God's free gift of grace makes us right with Him. Jesus paid the price to set us free!

How?

Even though we can't do anything to save ourselves from sin, we can be saved because of what Jesus has already done! By trusting Him with your life, you can live free from guilt and shame, knowing that YOU ARE LOVED!

If you're ready to accept God's gift and live LOVED, simply pray this prayer:

Dear Jesus, thank You for loving me and dying on the cross for my sins. Today I accept God's gift of salvation and I invite You to be the King of my heart. Please forgive me of my sins and guide me as I grow in friendship with You. Jesus, I want to be more like You and share Your love with others. Thank You that I don't have to be perfect but can grow in faith as I follow Your ways. In Your name I pray, amen.

WORD SEARCH!

```
F S H L Z M Q Z L W K A A S P L L B G
R Q H I S T O R Y T N Y U U R W E O B
P T A V S B D X F S G P J R O D L X Z
X A C T V P B M B A R N A B A S I S L
C Y L L D A W E J Z H C Z Q K L F A L
X S R S S N E U K G W I W E D G I E C
Y K A M L T D Y K A U T E Y R N T M Y
U L I O P Y S S A Q D I F W O I J A M
Z V X O C H V F B D N M A L L S F U I
W T H T X O V R F O H R O I T C H D D
T Y H H A S D K Q G A C E L Z B D A D
M U T I L E E Q C H I U Y N L N P N L
R A R E P R L D X O C A S S E R O L E
W W Z T N A K W P I I G O G R L I E T
A L U O L X S P U K E Y P E T E S B O
S D T W S E O A S Q I D I V M T A A W
A Z P N H A S I F B I A G E N T F K N
```

Middletown   Pantyhose
History   Colonial
Turtles   Wedgie
Casserole   FBI Agent
Quiz Bowl   PukeyPetes
Barnabas   SmoothieTown